"There's more, Lara... I haven't reached the part that includes you," Marc said.

Startled and curious, Lara stared at him.

"I've only told you part of my grandfather's demands. There's another part. I'm to marry this month and stay married for one year."

He reached across the table to take her hand, which was an action so unlike him that she nearly gasped. For a few seconds, she couldn't speak. She could only continue staring at him.

"Don't say anything until I'm through. You're surprised, just as I was when my grandfather told me."

While she heard his words, she was still focused on his hand wrapped around hers. It was warm, his grip light, yet the instant they touched, she tingled from head to toe.

Somehow, the touch of his hand had changed their relationship. She was certainly more aware of him as a man. And that awareness made it impossible to find words for a response.

He continued, "I want to see if I can make a deal with you...and make you my wife."

* * *

The Texan's Baby Proposal is part of the Callahan's Clan series—

A wealthy Texas family finds love under the Western skies!

Dear Reader,

How strong are the ties between grandparent and grandson or granddaughter? When I taught in the English department at a local university, I had a class on writing autobiographies. My students ranged in age from college freshmen to people who had retired and were taking college classes. I was surprised that the majority of students wrote about a grandparent as the most influential person in their lives. Maybe the reason I have grandparents in many of my books is because for all the early years of my life, I was close with my grandparents. Sometimes the love between grandparent and grandchild is one of the strongest of family ties, and that bond is the catalyst in this story to bring about life-changing events.

In order to fulfill his beloved grandfather's last wishes and gain a large inheritance, multimillionaire oilman and rancher Marc Medina opts for a marriage of convenience. This story is about two people who work together, deciding to take a chance on a paper marriage. When they wed and are out of the workplace, they discover new facets in each other. Set against the background of metropolitan Dallas and a cattle ranch in central Texas, this is the fourth story about the millionaire Callahans of Texas, their loves, their secrets and their friendships.

Thank you for your interest in my book.

Best wishes,

Sara Orwig

SARA ORWIG

THE TEXAN'S BABY PROPOSAL

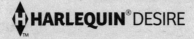

Recycling programs
for this product may
not exist in your area.

ISBN-13: 978-0-373-83862-2

The Texan's Baby Proposal

Printed in U.S.A.

Sara Orwig, from Oklahoma, loves family, friends, dogs, books, long walks, sunny beaches and palm trees. She is married to and in love with the guy she met in college. They have three children and six grandchildren. Sara's 100th published novel was a July 2016 release. With a master's degree in English, Sara has written historical romance, mainstream fiction and contemporary romance. Sara welcomes readers on Facebook or at saraorwig.com.

Books by Sara Orwig

Harlequin Desire

Lone Star Legends

The Texan's Forbidden Fiancée
A Texan in Her Bed
At the Rancher's Request
Kissed by a Rancher
The Rancher's Secret Son
That Night with the Rich Rancher

Callahan's Clan

Expecting the Rancher's Child
The Rancher's Baby Bargain
The Rancher's Cinderella Bride
The Texan's Baby Proposal

Visit her Author Profile page at Harlequin.com, or saraorwig.com, for more titles.

With many thanks to Stacy Boyd,
who made this book possible.
With thanks always to Maureen Walters.
Also with love to my family,
who fill my life with love and joy.

One

September

Facing a problem he never thought he would have, Marc Medina sat in his spacious Dallas office on a Tuesday evening and, through his open door, watched Lara Seymour, his executive secretary. It was almost an hour after closing time, but she had a six-o'clock appointment to talk to him. He knew she would appear promptly at six, not a minute early, not a minute late. He wondered what problem she had and hoped she wasn't planning to quit because she was the best secretary ever.

And the best looking.

He stifled that line of thought. CEO and President, Marc had built this company, Medina Energy. He had a policy of never dating a coworker, never getting emotionally involved with one, never flirting with one. Instead, he maintained a professional relationship at all times. Nothing would make him deviate from that policy, especially now that he was widowed.

Of all the women he had worked with, Lara was the biggest temptation. She was the only one he was keenly aware of as a woman. Still, their relationship had never gone beyond business friendly.

His thoughts returned to his ailing grandfather and his ultimatum to Marc—marry within this month and live on his grandfather's ranch for one year. If he did so, Marc and his mother stood to gain a large inheritance of mineral rights and producing wells, and he stood to gain the ranch. Marc wanted that inheritance and he wanted his mother to get hers, as well.

Knowing his grandfather, Marc was sure the old man figured that, since Marc dated some very beautiful ladies, he'd have no trouble getting a wife right away and then settling on the ranch. Marc knew what his grandfather ultimately wanted. Rico Ruiz's doctors had given him a limited time to live and he was no doubt making arrangements for his two greatest loves—his wife and his ranch. With Marc running the ranch, Rico would be reassured that his wife, Marc's grandmother, could live there in the house she was accustomed to for the rest of her days and Marc would care for her.

His grandfather had always thought Marc should live on the ranch. He thought Marc loved that life more than the corporate world, but as much as Marc did, he wasn't quite ready yet to be a rancher. He was sure his grandfather thought he knew what was best for his grandson. Marc loved the old man and he wanted to make his last days happy, so he'd try to do what his grandfather wished, but…

Where in blazes would he get a wife in a month? One he could tell goodbye later and dissolve the marriage.

That was the big catch. He didn't think any of the women he dated would want to marry and then split. He couldn't think of one woman friend he'd want to live with, even at the ranch where they had lots of space. He glanced at a short list of names on his desk. Each one already had a line drawn through it.

His attention was diverted as Lara passed the open door again. There went someone he could have around for one year. As a secretary, she was a huge help and yet she stayed in the background, usually barely noticeable, but always there when he needed her. Pity he couldn't ask her. He looked at his list of names again and wrote down another one, crossing it out as soon as he finished writing.

Searching his memory for anyone else, he glanced at Lara, who was seated at her desk putting something in a drawer. He suspected she was coming to see him to turn in her resignation. At her interview a year ago she'd mentioned she was saving her money to go to medical school someday. At the time he'd dismissed her statement as wishful thinking, but after working with her, he now believed what she said. When Lara set her mind to something, she got it done—fast and efficiently.

She reminded him of someone else he knew. Marc glanced at Kathy's picture on his desk and pulled it closer. "I miss you and need you," he whispered, thinking about his pregnant wife who'd died in a plane crash fourteen months earlier. It still hurt like hell to be without her. In that crash he lost his wife and his baby. Kathy had been two months pregnant.

He shifted his thoughts back to his ailing grandfather—another big, painful loss that was coming in his life. That made him think of his grandfather's ultimatum—or bargain, actually. Marc had two giant reasons for wanting to meet his grandfather's criteria. The first reason was that he wanted the ranch and the inheritance that would benefit not only him but his mother.

The other big reason was that he loved the old man. His grandfather had been the father figure in Marc's life since he was twelve years old and his dad died. Marc loved his grandpa and he wanted the man's last days to be happy ones. He wanted that with all his heart—he just hadn't known that would mean that he'd have to marry within a month.

"Damn," he said aloud, shaking his head and wondering what he was going to do. The stakes were too high and he loved his grandfather too much to say no to his proposition. But where was he going to find the perfect "wife"?

A knock on the door called a halt to his rambling thoughts. He looked at the clock. Six on the dot. As usual, Lara was right on time.

"Come in."

In a white cotton blouse with a tan tie at her throat and a matching tan skirt, she looked professional, tailored and so conservative she could easily fade into the background. In fact, there had been times she had to bring him papers during meetings and she had been barely noticeable, slipping in and out, a quiet, shadowy figure while so efficient at her job. Once again he hoped she wasn't going to quit. He knew she'd had a recent broken engagement, but he had never talked to her about it other than to say he was sorry. She had thanked him and only said she and her fiancé had had differences of opinions on some major issues.

Lara closed the door and turned back to him. "What I have to say is private and very personal."

He hid his surprise as he pointed at a chair in front of his desk. "Have a seat and tell me what's on your mind."

She had a graceful walk. Actually, she was damn attractive, with big blue eyes with amazingly thick, long lashes. She kept her dark brown hair in an upsweep; in fact, he'd never seen her with it down, falling free, but he imagined it was long and thick and luxuriant.

He gave her his full attention, curious about what was personal and important enough to warrant this meeting. She crossed her long legs, her tan skirt falling over her knees. She didn't need prompting but immediately began to speak.

"I have a situation that eventually I'll have to let everyone know about, but for now, it's private. I'll need to take some time off later."

"Sure, Lara. Whatever you need. We can fill in until you return," he said, relieved she wasn't quitting her job.

Her cheeks became flushed, adding to her looks. She wrung her hands and looked at the floor. The reaction surprised him because he had never seen her lose her poise or appear upset. She hadn't even appeared bothered by her broken engagement.

"I'm dealing with things I never had to deal with before and never expected to have happen in my life," she said, looking away as if lost in thought. "This is something I just never expected to have to discuss with my employer."

"Short of quitting your job, I doubt there's anything you really need to tell me. Unless you need help of some kind."

She gave him a fleeting smile that was gone in an

instant as she shook her head. "Oh, no. I don't need your help. Maybe just a little patience and understanding," she said with a tiny twist of her lips that she may have meant to be a smile.

"Lara, just say what it is. I'm not going to get angry. You're a great secretary."

With a deep breath she turned back to face him. "This is so hard, but I feel you should know."

"Go ahead and tell me if you think I should know," he said gently, wishing he could ease her discomfort.

She tightened her entwined fingers until her knuckles went white. "Oh, my," she said, looking away from him. When she turned back, her blue eyes gazed directly at him in a wide-eyed stare as she said bluntly, "I'm pregnant."

She drew in a deep breath and surged forward. "We didn't expect this to happen and Leonard Crane—my fiancé—really did not like it, so that's why we're no longer engaged." She paused a millisecond and went on.

"You see, my ex-fiancé didn't want children for a long time yet. He wanted me to get an abortion and I—well, I can't do that. I want my baby," she said with a note of fierce determination in her voice that startled him.

Marc understood now why she was so upset. No matter how much she wanted her baby, an unexpected pregnancy had to push her life off course. Lara was in such perfect control of every facet of her job and helped him keep control of his. She was efficient, intelligent, orderly, capable, dependable, driven. In fact, he was surprised that anything unplanned had occurred to her, especially a pregnancy.

He resisted the temptation to let his gaze drift over her figure, but he knew from the past few days of seeing her move around the office, she didn't show her condition at all. She was tall, probably five feet ten, and she was still slender.

"Is there anything I can do to help you?" he asked. He wondered if Lara needed money or a different place to live. He wondered if she had family to rely on. They had worked closely together and he thought a lot of her. He'd do whatever he could to help her and her baby.

She merely shook her head and gave him a small, forced smile to reassure him she was okay. Instead, it only made him aware of her good looks again.

And that's when the thought hit him. Lara had a dilemma…and he had a dilemma. She was pregnant, working to support herself and to save for her education. He needed a temporary wife to win his inheritance. Perhaps he had a solution to help them both out…

Would she be a candidate for a marriage of convenience?

He had no doubt Lara would be willing to dissolve the marriage later. That was the best thing of all. She had her own agenda, plus the drive, the willpower and the stamina to stick with it. In a temporary marriage of convenience, she wouldn't make demands on him or expect him to fall in love. He couldn't. His heart was still with his wife. He hadn't gotten over her loss and he wasn't ready for another relationship.

He'd been able to work closely with Lara for a year without ever crossing that line and getting personal. He knew he'd be able to keep their relationship the same as it had been.

In the meantime, he could give her the financial support that would take away a lot of her worries about her baby.

Yes, the more he thought about it, the more appealing the idea became.

He wasn't aware she was even speaking until she shifted in her seat and drew his attention.

"If I continue to feel good, I'll work until it's time for my baby, if that's all right with you."

"It'll certainly be fine with me. You take the time you need for leave," he hoped he said. His thoughts were still on the prospect that she actually might be a good candidate for a short-term marriage. Again, he thought about that awareness he had of her as an attractive woman. Would that make it more difficult to keep his distance in a marriage of convenience than it had in the office? He didn't think it would.

The more he mulled over the thought, the more he knew. Lara Seymour was the answer to his dilemma.

He tried to pay attention as she talked about her

plans, but his thoughts could not be corralled. He was so sure of his plan that he wanted to pose the offer right away. But he couldn't do that here in the office. No, he'd rather get his offer lined up in his own thoughts and ask her to dinner to tell her. Somewhere private where they would not be interrupted.

"I'm only in my second month, actually not far into my second month, so this is very early. I'd prefer not to announce this to the office, which is why I wanted to see you after hours."

"Of course. I won't mention it. I appreciate you letting me know, even though I won't need to get someone to fill in for you for months yet."

"I thought it only fair to tell you now. So far I feel fine, so that's good."

"That's very good," he said, smiling at her. "Lara, you don't need to answer if you don't want to, but I really know nothing about your private life. Do you have family here who will be with you?"

She gazed at him with a solemn look that was so unlike her, he was startled. She shook her head. "I have friends. I don't have relatives. My mom died of leukemia when I was eighteen. I had an older sister who died of acute leukemia when she was seven. My dad walked out when I was a little kid. I don't remember him or know him. There are no relatives."

Marc was shocked, but tried to hide his surprise. "I'm so sorry. I didn't know that. I know you have friends and a lot of them here in this office. People like you."

He couldn't stop thinking of her being so alone. He had never known anyone who had no living relatives. He was so locked into his relationships with his family, he couldn't imagine her solitary situation. She needed his help so much more than he had thought and it made him feel better to think that he could be a huge help to her and her baby. If this had been his wife, he would hope someone would have helped her.

He could set up a trust for Lara's baby. He could let the baby have his name. If they married now, most people would assume he was the father, which would be fine with him because it would help her.

"I have wonderful friends here. This is a great office and a great place to work," she said, giving him a radiant smile. Idly, he wondered how many single guys in his office had tried to date her.

"You have a master's degree. When you came to work here, you told me you wanted to work to save enough money to go to medical school. Is that still on your agenda?" he asked.

"Oh, yes. My pregnancy is a setback, but I still intend to pursue my dreams. I want to go into medical research someday. With my mother's illness I saw that there is still so much to be discovered about such diseases. If I can do anything to help in that field, I want to, for my mother's memory. Doctors just couldn't do anything to save her, but medical science makes new discoveries constantly. I want to help people. If I don't get into medical school, I can do something else to help others."

"That's commendable. I hope you get to carry out your plans," he said, thinking he should be able to help her meet some of her financial needs for her education.

"It will take me a little longer to earn and save the money to go back to school, but I intend to do so. If I can get accepted into medical school, I definitely plan to go. If not, I'll become a chemist."

"That's tough without family members to help and to babysit."

"I'll manage," she replied with a lift of her chin.

"I'm sure you will," he said, and meant it. It hadn't taken long to recognize her drive and ambition after she came to work for him. He'd seen it in himself and his mother all his life.

"If you don't feel well, I want you to stay home. If you're already here and don't feel well, please don't keep working. Take off and tell me if you need help getting home or anything."

She smiled again. "Thanks. That's nice but I'll be all right. I've been fine so far. Not even morning sickness."

"That's good. I assume you have a doctor."

"Oh, yes, I have a doctor who came with lots of recommendations from friends." She smiled at him. "Well…I guess there's nothing more to say but thank you for being so cooperative and helpful. I'll let you know when I tell anyone else in the office and this is no longer a secret. It can't be a secret for long," she said, forcing a smile. Then she stood up, and as she did, his gaze swept over her and he liked what he saw. Her white blouse revealed full curves and a tiny waist.

There were moments—like this one—when he forgot her secretarial status and their business relationship, but he always caught himself before he said or did anything to indicate he saw her as an attractive woman instead of his very competent secretary. He caught himself again now, going to open the door for her.

"Take care of yourself and, again, if you need anything or don't feel well, don't hesitate to tell me," he repeated. She turned to face him and suddenly he was aware of how close they stood. His gaze shifted to her full lips and he felt a tightening deep inside. For just a flash, he saw a flicker of her lashes and her cheeks became a deeper pink.

"Thanks, Marc. You're always understanding," she said softly and hurried out, crossing the room to her desk, which had everything in its proper place and ready for the next morning. She opened a drawer, retrieved her purse and turned to smile at him again. "I'll see you in the morning."

"Sure," he said, still watching her as she walked away.

He turned, walked back to his desk and sat, seeing the glass door to the outer office close behind her.

It always surprised him when he noticed her, because he still mourned his wife and he didn't pay attention to women the way he had before his marriage. Even though in the past few months he had started taking women friends out, he would never be serious about any of them. In fact, he wasn't even interested in any of them.

He thought about Lara.

And the more he thought about her, the more he knew she was the perfect "wife." He hadn't gotten over Kathy and wasn't ready for any kind of relationship, but Lara wouldn't expect one. She wouldn't want to fall in love any more than he wanted to, because she had other plans for her future. And while he stood to gain from this crazy marriage of convenience, so would she. She'd reap the reward of the help he could give her and her baby—not only in a trust he'd set up for the child but in giving the baby his name.

No doubt about it, Lara was the right person to ask.

Well, maybe there was one doubt...

For an instant he thought of the moments when he'd had to bank an electrifying awareness of her as an appealing woman. Could he push aside that attraction? He had to, because Lara and he would both get what they wanted from the marriage. He'd get the ranch and she'd get the financial and maybe emotional support she needed for this pregnancy. Then, when they dissolved the marriage, they'd go their separate ways and both be happy about it and much better off because of the marriage of convenience.

Meanwhile, he knew he could live with her and still continue their business relationship. After all, they didn't need to go to bed with each other. He hadn't gotten over the loss of his wife, and she had just broken an engagement.

No matter how he looked at it, marriage to Lara would benefit both of them, as well as his family. It would benefit Lara's baby, too. And some part of him wanted that. Somehow, helping the baby pleased him a lot and made him feel closer to the little baby of his own that he had lost.

He looked up Lara's number, picked up his phone and called to invite her to dinner.

By half past six Wednesday evening, Lara was ready and waiting. She had dressed just as conservatively as she did at the office, in a black, long-sleeved dress with a high round neckline and straight skirt. But as she took a final glance at herself in the mirror, she noticed the dress was shorter and dressier than anything she'd worn to the office. She told herself it was the perfect compromise for a dinner date with her boss. She couldn't imagine why he had asked her out.

When he'd called last night he hadn't made it sound as if this was social. At the same time, it wasn't business related or he would have told her.

She had accepted his dinner invitation knowing she'd find out the reason soon enough.

She tried to ignore the flutters in her belly when she thought of dining with her boss. Marc was handsome, charming, capable, a strong, sexy man—something she tried to avoid thinking about most of the time. She had heard all the office talk—how his pregnant wife of three months had died in a plane crash and he still mourned her and had no interest in any other woman.

She suspected he was smart enough to avoid getting sexually or emotionally involved with anyone at work.

She was attracted to him and had been from the first moment she met him, but she'd resisted with all her being because at first there was no future in it and later she became engaged. His heart was locked away, and even if it wasn't, she had plans for her life. Plans that did not call for her to get romantically involved with her boss, no matter how good-looking he was. Still, what was the harm in admitting that the man was handsome and had sex appeal? Bushels of it. In fact, sometimes she found it difficult to keep remote, professional and cool around him. Nevertheless, she did.

Thinking about him, she sighed. Surely Marc wasn't taking her out tonight to let her go. He wouldn't do that. As for his motives, she'd know in a matter of minutes.

She took one last look in the mirror. Her hair was looped and pinned up on her head, just the way she wore it at work today. Her makeup was light but flawless, optimally highlighting her blue eyes and high cheekbones. As she gazed into the mirror, her mind must have started playing tricks on her, because she suddenly saw Marc's image beside her. His thick, black, unruly hair, slightly tanned skin, the shadow of stubble on his jaw and his thickly lashed dark brown eyes. He stood next to her, over six feet tall, broad shouldered and strong, and he reached out to touch her and—

Her thoughts were interrupted by the sound of a car door closing. In seconds her doorbell rang. She took a deep breath and hurried to answer it. She swung it open to face her boss and her heart lurched.

Dressed in a navy suit and red tie that she had seen before, he looked handsome. She smiled, but felt odd flutters and she assumed it was because it seemed so much like a date. She banished that thought and looked up at him. "Do you want to come in?"

"Thanks, but we have reservations shortly, and I think we better go."

"I'm more than happy to go have dinner with you, Marc, but I'm a little puzzled as to why we're doing this. I don't feel as if it's a social event."

He smiled at her. "Smart woman. I have something I want to talk to you about and I want to be away from the office and away from interruptions."

"Ahhh," she said, nodding. While that clarified their dinner engagement slightly, she still had questions. She suspected his "something" concerned work because his office manner hadn't changed from what it had been all day. "I'll get my purse," she said, stepping back into her entryway briefly before joining him.

She closed her door and heard the lock click into place. As she walked beside him to the car, she was acutely conscious of how close he was and how tall he was. She had far more physical awareness of him now that they were out of the routine office setting, but his demeanor was the same. He didn't take her arm as they walked to the car. He didn't touch her in any way. So why couldn't she stop the prickly awareness that plagued her?

She told herself to pretend she was in the office, that it was just lunch together on a weekday. That didn't work.

He held the car door and she slid into the seat. She watched him walk around the car, the wind blowing unruly locks of his curly hair. What did he have to talk to her about here that he couldn't discuss at the office?

Her curiosity mushroomed when they went to a town club where he was a member. Inside, they were taken to a private room.

"Now I am curious about tonight," she said as she sat across from him.

He merely nodded. "Let's get our drinks and order dinner before we talk. I don't want any interruptions.

But I will tell you this is personal and involves my grandfather."

Startled, she couldn't imagine what could concern her and involve his very ill grandfather. "There's no guessing why I'm here having dinner with you if it involves Mr. Ruiz. That lets out anything regarding the office."

"Not altogether," Marc said. "I have a proposition I want you to consider."

Her curiosity reached a fevered peak but she reined in her questions when the waiter came to ask their drink preferences. Marc ordered sparkling water for her and a martini for himself.

She sat quietly until finally they had ordered dinner and been served their drinks. He raised his glass in a toast.

"Here's to the best secretary I've ever worked with and, hopefully, to a mutually bright future together."

She touched her glass to his and sipped, watching him and waiting as he set his martini on the table. Her curiosity increased because, whatever he was about to discuss, it involved both of their futures.

He folded his hands on the table and cleared his throat. "I'll cut to the chase now. My grandfather is very ill with pancreatic cancer and doctors have given him three months to live."

"I'm sorry," she said, hearing the pain in Marc's voice even though he seemed in control of his emotions.

"I'm close to him. My dad died when I was twelve and my grandfather has always been there for me. I've spent a lot of time with my grandparents on their ranch. I love that life and I love that ranch. It's beautiful." He smiled at her. "At least, it is to me."

"I'm sorry, Marc, that your grandfather's health isn't good," she said, still unable to see how any of this involved her.

"Thanks. My grandparents love that ranch. They've worked it all their lives."

He paused when the waitstaff came in with their dinners—a thick steak for Marc and Alaskan salmon for her. When they were alone again, she had a bite of salmon and closed her eyes. "Mmm, this is delicious."

"Yes, it is," he said, his voice deeper than usual. She opened her eyes to see him watching her. Heat flashed through her and she was aware of the intense way he looked at her. His dark brown eyes hid his feelings.

"Go ahead with your story," she said, suddenly tingling with awareness. She knew whatever he was going to ask her, it had nothing to do with the office. Not with the look she had just received from him.

He took a deep breath and nodded. "Now that my grandfather is ill, he's worried about my grandmother. She wants to stay on the ranch and live out her life there, but—this is where I come in—she can't run it or deal with it herself. And this is where you come in." He paused and nodded at her plate. "Maybe you should enjoy a few more bites of dinner before I continue."

She shook her head. "My curiosity will overcome me." She wondered if he was thinking about trying to hire her as a companion for his grandmother. "What on earth is it, that I won't be able to eat after you tell me?"

"I think I'm going to shock you. Frankly, I'm still reeling in shock myself," he said, forcing a smile at her. "My grandfather wants me to move to the ranch and I have to agree to stay at least one year. That way I'll be there to see that my grandmother is all right."

"You're leaving the company for a year?" Lara asked. "Or will it be longer?" Was she losing her boss permanently? She felt a pang at the thought and immediately thought of his vice presidents, wondering whom she would work for.

"It'll only be a year. I know my grandpa and how he thinks. He thinks if I live out there a year, I'll never want to leave."

"I can understand what he wants, but is that what you want to do?"

"He's given me an offer—actually, it's more an ultimatum. I live there a year and I inherit the ranch, also one third of the mineral rights and one third of the producing wells on the ranch. My mother will also inherit a third, the same as I will, and the remainder of the estate will go to my grandmother."

"I see." She put down her fork and wiped her lips on her napkin. "You wanted to tell me that I'll have a new boss."

"Oh, no. I'm not through. I love my grandfather too much to refuse to do what he wants. Even if I didn't feel that way, this offer is too big to turn down. And I love that ranch. As I said, I love Grandpa and I want his last days to be happy. I want to do what he wants and make him happy."

"That's wonderful, Marc. I can understand. I loved my mother, and at the last, I did everything I could to make her happy. I'll miss working for you," she said, hoping she didn't sound too depressed, but she would miss him terribly. She liked working for him. He was a fair, considerate boss and a handsome, appealing man, so it was nice to be around him.

"There's more, Lara, but I'm trying to wait until you've had enough of your dinner that you won't go home hungry."

She picked up her fork again, to placate him, and smiled up at him. "I'm eating, okay? But you've told me your news—that you're leaving."

"I haven't reached the part that includes you," he reminded her.

Startled, she stared at him as curiosity gripped her. Maybe he wanted a secretary on the ranch. Was that it?

"Lara, I've only told you part of my grandfather's

demands. There's another part. Besides living on the ranch for a year, I'm to marry this month."

He reached across the table to take her hand, which was something so unlike him that she nearly gasped. For a few seconds, she couldn't speak. She could only stare at him.

"Don't say anything until I'm through. You're surprised, just as I was."

While she heard his words, she was still focused on his hand wrapped around hers. His hand was warm, his grip light, yet the instant they touched she tingled from head to toe. Somehow, she felt the touch of his hand had changed their relationship in a subtle way. She was certainly more aware of him as a man. And that awareness made it impossible to respond.

"I need a wife for a marriage of convenience, possibly for one year, possibly much shorter," he continued. "In order to inherit, I have to marry this month and live on the ranch for one year. That is what my grandfather has in his will. I want a wife as long as my grandfather is alive, which doctors have only given him a few months. I want his last days happy. After he is gone, I will stay on the ranch that full year, but there is nothing in his will about how long I have to stay married. When he is gone, I will end the marriage—that's a promise," he said. "I want to see if I can make a deal with you. Make you my wife."

Two

Stunned, she stared at him, looking into unfathomable brown eyes that hid his feelings so well. Marry Marc and then dissolve it? She couldn't imagine doing such a thing. Those dark eyes so intently focused on her took her breath away. Marry Marc. Without love. A marriage for convenience. Her heart raced at the thought.

"Marc, that's very flattering, but I can't do that," she said, her pulse pounding. *Marry* Marc? For a moment she felt light-headed. She couldn't agree to what he was proposing.

"Wait a minute. Just listen to the whole thing. What's in this for me, and more importantly, what's in this for you. Please, just listen."

"I am," she said. Breathless, still in such shock, she could only stare at him, trying to hear and process what he was saying.

"You haven't heard my part of this bargain. I stand to get big financial gains if I do what my grandfather wants. And I'll inherit his ranch—a fine, working ranch. But, Lara, I intend for this deal to benefit the woman I marry, also."

She gazed into eyes so dark they were almost black and knew that, whatever the outcome, she would remember this moment and what he had just said to her for the rest of her life. She had a feeling that her life might be about to change in a manner she had never envisioned. If she married him. She couldn't imagine that happening.

"You and I are compatible," he said. "We're able to be together and we know we can work together. I want to help you in your endeavors and help you take care of your baby. I want to give you and your baby a great start in your new life. I want to give your baby security and legitimacy—my name. If you'll marry me in this marriage of convenience, I'll draw up the papers and give you two hundred thousand dollars when we marry and two hundred thousand when we divorce. After my grandfather is gone, I want us both free."

"That's staggering, Marc," she whispered, so stunned by his offer that she could only stare at him. "That's almost half a million dollars," she whispered.

"I can go to school and I won't have to work in the office."

"That's right. As much as I hate to lose you as a secretary, I need you more in this."

"But you go out and have women friends. Why are you asking me? We haven't even dated."

"This isn't a marriage made from a romance. It's a marriage of convenience and my grandfather just required that I live on the ranch for one year. When my grandfather is gone, I want to return to my single status—and I will," Marc said, giving her a direct look that spoke volumes about his determination to do just that. "The women I take to parties and concerts and shows—I don't think any of them would go into a marriage with the agreement that it would be over, maybe in several months."

"I can see that," she said without thinking, and his lips curved in a faint smile.

"You, on the other hand, have an agenda. You plan on medical school and you'll have a baby. I think you'll be willing to walk away from this when we divorce."

"Will we…will we live as man and wife?" she asked. "Including sex?"

"If that's your preference, yes, we can. If it's not—and since this marriage is definitely temporary—I think we can manage. We did well working together for the past year. This should be even easier because we won't see each other on a daily basis the way we have at the office. I still love and miss my wife. I'm not interested in a relationship."

"I just broke an engagement and I'm not interested in one, either," she said, her cheeks turning pink.

"Then that settles that question. We'll continue in a friendly manner the way we did at the office. This way, we won't have emotional complications," he said, smiling at her, and she smiled in return. "It's not something that can't be changed if we decide we want to change it," he added, and she nodded.

"Marc, I have to admit I'm stunned. I can't believe what you're offering."

"Think about it, Lara. You're alone now, but you won't be if you take this offer. I can help you so you can take care of yourself and your baby, get that education you want so you can save some lives or help others in some way. You'll be helping my mother and me get this inheritance. It's mutually beneficial and I hope changes your life for the better."

"Of course it will," she answered. She stared at him and he gazed back in silence. Could she live under the same roof with him without falling into bed with him? Could she live with him and not get emotionally involved? He was a sexy, desirable man. And she knew he could do far more damage to her heart than she'd experienced this past year, and that had been terrible.

"Lara, I'm sure people at the office have talked to you about my wife. You've seen her picture on my desk. She was pregnant with our baby when she was killed in a plane crash after we had been married three months. We had been married three months, four days, fourteen hours to be exact." He looked away, and when he talked, his voice was flat.

"I'm sorry, Marc, for your loss."

"I loved her," he said quietly, and Lara wondered if he had forgotten her presence and was caught in memories. She sat quietly as he drew a deep breath.

"Enough of that, except to say, I will not make this marriage permanent, nor will it become personal. I still love Kathy and miss her with all my being. I know I need to get over my loss, but that hasn't happened and I want to be up front and honest with you."

"I understand. My broken engagement hurt me and left me not trusting my judgment in men. I get it. But I also know you well, since we've worked closely together for the past year."

"I want to help you, especially since you don't have any family," he said. "In addition to what I've offered, there are some other things."

"There's more?" she asked in surprise.

"Oh, yes. In addition to giving your child my name, I'll set up a two-hundred-thousand-dollar trust fund for your baby."

"Whoever agrees to this marriage will become wealthy. You're willing to give me a fortune and my child your name?" she repeated, knowing she had to accept his offer.

"Yes, I am, because of what I'll inherit from my grandfather. It'll make his last days happier ones, and it will change my mother's life for the better. And I hope it will change yours, as well."

"That's incredibly generous."

"I'll be on the ranch, but when the year is up, I'll have someone else run the ranch and have a companion and help for my grandmother, and I'll return to Dallas and the corporate world. I'll retire later to the ranch."

Still in shock, she sat quietly, her head spinning. "Marc, I can't even absorb this. My life will change totally."

"Yes, it will." His hand tightened around hers. "Lara, I want the ranch and my grandfather's inheritance, and I need this marriage. And I don't want him to be unhappy in his last days. I love him," Marc said gruffly, and impulsively, she squeezed his hand.

"I'm sorry. It hurts to lose someone you love. I know," she said quietly.

She started to pull her hand away, but he held it. "You have soft hands," he said quietly.

She realized they had been circumspect at the office, never even touching. But now his hand on hers was electrifying. For a moment she forgot his proposition, her dinner, everything else except his hand holding hers.

His gaze met hers. "We've worked together well. We can do this. Your engagement is broken. You have your plans for your future. We can help each other."

Her insides trembled again. She was intensely aware of him, yet still trying to grasp the amount of money that could be hers if she accepted his offer. The temptation was great to accept instantly, yet years of caution and self-control caused her to remain silent.

"I'm surprised I didn't faint. I have to think about this."

"How many times in your life have you fainted?"

"None," she answered, startled by his question until she saw his smile.

"I didn't think so. Look, Lara, I know it's a shock. I've been in shock to find out I have to marry this month. I want you to think this over."

"I've worked with you for almost a year now and I've seen you in a lot of different situations. You're one of the good guys, Marc. I feel I can trust you." She diverted her gaze a moment, then looked back into his eyes, deeply and sincerely. "Since I feel that way, with the offer you've made, I can't possibly turn it down. Yes, Marc, I'll marry you in a marriage of convenience that we know will end."

"I'll still give you a little time to think about this and back out if you want. I hope you don't back out, but I don't want a quick decision when this is a life changer. You don't know what I'm like away from the office. We should go out together a few times before we're locked into this."

He released her hand and she wondered if he had given the contact any thought. "All good ideas, Marc." Her mind reeled with questions. "Your grandmother has a house there, right? Or will she live in the same house with us? Oh, my heavens! *With us*—that sounds so impossible," she said breathlessly while she gazed into his eyes. *I'm going to marry Marc. I'm going to be his wife.* The thoughts swirled and she could feel her face flush. "I can't imagine any of this."

"See why I wanted you to eat some of your dinner?" he asked. "You haven't eaten a bite since I told you why I asked you out."

"You were right. My appetite is gone. The dinner is delicious, but my head is spinning and my stomach is churning." She grasped his hand again. His hand was warm and solid, and her reaction to the physical contact was just as electrifying as before. She was conscious that his fingers closed gently around hers.

"Damn, your hand is cold as ice," he said and clutched it between both of his.

"I'm in shock and nervous and excited. This is something I never dreamed would happen. I'm excited, scared, flattered—countless reactions that keep shifting and changing with each breath I take. Right now, the money is dazzling, but I know I have to look beyond the money. The prospect of us being married—that's shocking and something I've never considered."

He leaned closer across the table. "I understand some of your feelings. That's exactly why I said you should take some time to think about your answer," he said, brushing loose strands of her hair away from her face. His touch was feathery, except it was Marc and she was acutely aware of him. He gazed at her intently and his steady look took her breath away. What were these intense reactions she was having to him? She didn't have those at the office. But at the office, she had never had to consider marriage to him, even if it wasn't forever, wasn't out of love and wasn't even real.

"I'll do that if you want, but the offer you just made to me—I don't have to think about what I want to do. You'll solve so many of my problems for me," she said, leaning closer to him and lowering her voice. "I'll say goodbye to you when we divorce, so I can go on with my dream to become a doctor and to go into medical research."

They both leaned over the table, till mere inches separated them. She searched his gaze, yet his eyes revealed nothing of what was truly going on in his head.

He looked intently at her and then his gaze lowered to her mouth.

She tingled all over and drew a deep breath. She could practically feel his lips on hers as he looked at her mouth. Without thinking she ran her tongue over her lower lip, realized what she was doing and closed her mouth, looking up to meet his knowing gaze. When she felt the heat in her cheeks, she knew she had blushed.

"Our boss-and-secretary relationship just went up in smoke," she whispered, and he nodded.

"Absolutely."

For a moment he was silent, staring at her lips, then just like a rogue wind, the moment was swept away. Slowly he sat back and she followed suit, feeling bereft after his near kiss.

"You were the best secretary I could've wished for," he said finally. "But that's gone for good. I need you more for this marriage of convenience because that's a role almost impossible to fill."

"You just changed my life forever, for the better. You've given me and my baby opportunities in life."

"We'll get to know each other," he said in a husky voice. Then, as if he'd suddenly thought of a pressing question, he asked, "When is your baby due?"

"Next April."

"If we plan to stay together for a year, I'll be there for those early months when I can help while you get settled into motherhood."

She smiled at him.

"If we marry, even if it is just a bargain marriage, we'll be thrown into close, constant contact—although it's a big house. Just remember, Lara, I won't change my mind. This marriage will never turn into something permanent, which I know you don't want, anyway."

"No, I don't. I know from the start that it's a business deal and it's temporary. I can deal with that."

"I'm sure you can," he remarked dryly. "I just wanted you to clearly understand my feelings. I don't want you hurt by this or having a broken heart. I feel as if my heart turned to stone when I lost my wife. You don't even have to stay on the ranch all the time. I'd like you around some of the time while my grandfather is alive. I just want him happy."

"I know. Losing someone you love hurts badly," she answered. "Remember, I lost my mother and I had an engagement shattered and it hurt. I don't want to go through that again, so I'll be careful."

"If you accept, and you sound as if you plan to accept, I don't care what kind of wedding we have. I'll leave that up to you. Whatever you want is fine. I can pay for it. It just has to be soon. I mean, like next week or the week after at the latest. I don't want any last-minute thing. With Grandpa's health the way it is, the sooner our wedding, the better."

"The sooner the better. Oh, my. My head is spinning. I can't believe all this. One thing. I'm enrolled in a night class this semester. The doctor said it's fine. The class ends in December."

"Lara, you said you don't have any relatives. Who's closest to you? Who will you tell about this?"

"There's my friend Melanie, and Patsy from work,

and some friends in my neighborhood, including an older couple next door who think they're substitute grandparents. Mr. and Mrs. Vickers."

"We really don't have long to pull a wedding together. I want you to think everything over tonight and give me an answer tomorrow. You're saying yes now, but I want you to be sure," he said.

"I am so sure, Marc," she said. "I promise you, I'm ready to accept your offer. And I will get out of the marriage, just as surely as you want to."

"You don't want to sleep on it?"

Aware she was changing her future, her life, her baby's life, she shook her head. "My answer to your proposal is yes."

"Then I'll have my lawyer draw up an agreement and a prenup. If you back out, you forfeit everything except one hundred dollars that will be a token."

"Fine," she said. They sat gazing at each other, and her heartbeat quickened as she looked into his eyes. His hand covered hers again.

"We're getting married," he whispered. "We're not in love, but we can get to know each other a little better and let the friendship grow. We've always gotten along and worked well together as boss and secretary. And now we have decisions to make as a couple—wedding decisions, decisions about when you quit your job, when we announce our engagement, a lot of things. Can you go to dinner tomorrow night?" He smiled suddenly. "Maybe then I won't send you into shock and you'll get to eat your meal."

"Yes, I can."

He nodded at her plate. "Want your dinner now?"

She shook her head. "I can't eat a bite. I'm too excited. Actually, I'd like to take a walk. By now the weather outside should have cooled some and I feel like I need to move around."

"Let's go. They'll put dinner on my tab. We don't need to wait."

He stood and held her chair as she rose. When she turned, she faced him and they were only inches apart. Her pulse jumped and she felt riveted, unable to move at all.

Our boss-and-secretary relationship just went up in smoke.

She remembered her words from a moment ago and realized how true they really were. Going forward, their relationship would be different. *Very different*, she thought, barely able to catch her breath. She had always tried to keep her distance and squelch any physical reaction she had to him. She had always avoided physical contact. Now they would be husband and wife. Even though it was in name only, nothing would ever be the same.

Shocking her almost as much as his proposal was a sudden, intense awareness of him, far beyond anything she had ever felt before. His eyes narrowed the barest fraction, but she noticed, and she felt as

SARA ORWIG   43

if sparks flew between them. A sizzling attraction made her want to lean toward him, to touch him. Her lips tingled and her gaze lowered to his mouth as she wondered what it would be like to kiss him.

How could their coming change invoke this hot attraction so swiftly?

She needed to get back her detached business personality and keep a wall between them. That's what both of them wanted. This would not be a marriage made in love and she needed to guard her heart all the time because he clearly would not fall in love and she didn't want to fall in love—or fall into his bed, either.

With an effort she stepped away from him.

He took her arm and they left the club, turning on the sidewalk in downtown Dallas. How long would it be before she would get accustomed to him touching her? She had a prickly awareness of how close he was when he took her arm to cross the street. People were still out, but she was conscious of no one and nothing except him. His height as he walked beside her, his hand grazing hers as they strolled. Was she stepping into a situation where she would have a bigger heartbreak than ever? When she'd ended her engagement, she had been the one who wanted out of the relationship. This time, Marc would end the relationship, so she needed to be careful to protect her heart and stay out of his bed.

"I don't know much about your private life," she

said. "If I'm going to marry you, I think you better tell me, at least briefly."

"Sure. I was born in Downly, Texas."

She smiled. "You don't have to start that far back."

With a flash of even, white teeth, he grinned. "My mom's family all came from Mexico because of relatives in Downly. Are you familiar with Downly?"

"I've heard of it, but I've never been there."

"Mom and her family got jobs there and their citizenship. My mom got a job as a maid for a wealthy family. Actually, it was Dirkson Callahan."

Startled, she looked up at him. "Oh, my. You're about to buy some of his wells in South Dakota. You told me at the office that it was routine business. I know you're close friends with his son, Gabe Callahan, but will buying the wells be something more personal?"

"You've already moved into the fiancée mode. You wouldn't have asked me that at the office," he said, sounding amused again.

"Are you going to be one of those men who's got everything bottled up and keeps a lot to yourself? Maybe I should learn the parameters here."

He laughed and put his arm around her to squeeze her shoulder as they walked. "I'm teasing you. Gabe always thought Dirkson was an uncaring dad. He didn't keep up with his boys or share in their lives. None of them were happy with him. I talked to Gabe about it before I did anything, and he said it wouldn't mean anything to his dad or any of them if I bought those wells and to go ahead. So I am. And you can ask whatever you want."

"Oh, really?" she said, stopping to put her hand on her hip, unable to resist flirting with him.

"Oh, yeah," he answered in a husky voice, his eyes twinkling, and her pulse jumped. "What very private thing would you like to know?"

She caught her lower lip with her teeth as she thought for a few seconds. "Am I ever going to get breakfast in bed?"

"If you're in our bed, you will," he answered.

"You are quick. I'll remember that."

"So will I," he said in a deeper voice. They looked at each other and both laughed.

When they did, he hugged her lightly again. "I'm liking this deal better by the minute."

"Don't get excited. You're accustomed to me being your secretary and doing whatever you ask. That isn't necessarily going to happen when I become your wife."

He leaned closer, tilting her chin up with his forefinger and gazing at her. "Then I'll just have to butter you up so I get my way."

She smiled when he did and they turned to continue walking. "Does your mom still work for him?" Lara asked.

"No. She quit to open a small tamale stand and tiny café—I mean, really small. This was before I was born, so I know little about it. My mom met my dad and I think it must have been love at first sight. They were married three weeks after they met and they loved each other deeply. He was a good dad, too. He had immigrated to the US earlier, gotten his citizenship and had a job. He worked in construction. He really wasn't a strong man and shouldn't have been doing that."

"You don't take after him there," she said without thinking about it.

"I didn't know I'd exhibited any great stamina in the office," Marc said, sounding amused and looking down at her.

"You carry things around sometimes. I've seen you do things. I'm observant," she said, aware her cheeks were suddenly hot.

"Oh, yeah?" He touched her arm as he stepped in front of her again. "Maybe I should ask what else you know about me from observation."

She thought a moment. "You send roses to women you've been out with, and if it's someone a little more special, you send a big mixed bouquet. Right?"

"Damn. I must be as predictable as hell. How did you figure that out?" He stared at her.

"That's a guess. The mixed bouquet has roses. The lady who gets the mixed bouquet gets roses plus other flowers."

"Well, you're right." He nodded and they continued walking.

"Go on about your family," she urged him. "I don't know anything about them."

"When my family moved to Texas, they didn't have money, but they were successful. Mom's little café grew and when my dad's health began to fail, as long as he could, he helped in the café. By that time, my grandfather was doing better and he put some money into her café. Then my dad's health got worse and he had heart problems. I had wonderful parents and wonderful grandparents and I'm sorry you lost your family so early in life. It hurt to lose my dad and it's going to hurt like hell to lose Grandpa."

She grasped Marc's hand and squeezed lightly, releasing him swiftly and trying to ignore the inevitable tingles. "I know, Marc. I was so close to my mother."

"When I lost my dad, I got closer to my grandfather on Mom's side. He was the father figure in my life after Dad was gone."

"You had a lot of family."

"My mom's dad worked for a successful rancher and moved up to become foreman. On that side of the family I come from people who are driven and work hard. My mom put work first in her life always. So did Grandpa. Sometimes I think they both worked too much. The man who owned the ranch didn't have children. When the rancher's wife died, he willed the ranch to my grandfather and four years later, when the rancher died, Grandpa inherited it. I was seven years old then and already loved to visit my grandparents. It's a great ranch."

She noticed his voice changed and she wondered how much he liked ranching versus working in Dallas in an office.

That question and others would have to wait. She was getting tired of walking and her feet were killing her in her heels. She looked at her surroundings. "I'm not familiar with where we are now and we've walked quite a way."

He swung her around and they headed back as she laughed. "Oooh, I get what I want the minute I ask. I'm going to like my new role."

He stopped and faced her. Surprised, she looked up at him as wind caught locks of his dark, curly hair.

"I'm beginning to look forward to our deal. And we better get on with it. So, we're on for dinner tomorrow night?"

"Yes, thank you. We need to make wedding plans if you want to move so fast."

He stepped beside her again and they continued walking. "Think of the secretaries in the office. Is there anyone who'd be a good replacement? If we can find someone who's already working there, it'll be easier for you to train them before you leave."

"You have two who should be perfect. They're quiet about their work and I don't think most people realize how much they get done. Let me think about that tonight before I give you names. But you should know you've got good employees."

"That's what I like to hear."

By the time they walked back to his car and drove to her house, the sun was setting in the western sky. When they walked up onto her porch, Marc stepped between her and the door. Surprised, she looked up at him, suddenly feeling caught in the depths of his brown eyes.

"Definitely, I've made a good choice here," he said in husky tones that gave her a tingle.

"And I know I made a good decision in accepting your offer. You've solved so many problems in my life. My world will change, thanks to you. The thing we need to remember is you have plans and I have plans. I've had my goals since the first six months of my mom's illness. I don't intend to give them up. I got engaged and we thought we could work it out, but we didn't plan on a baby. This baby is part of me and my mom and my family, and I'm not giving it up. Now I'll be free to get my education. I feel I owe that to my mom."

"That's one reason you were such a good choice. You have an agenda. You won't want to stay married. Even if we get along great, you'll want to go to med school and I won't want a wife who is wrapped up in school and becoming a doctor. Besides,you know, Lara, that I still love my wife and I'm not over that loss."

"I understand that. You know you have to let go, but part of you can't ever let go when it's someone you love," she said solemnly.

He nodded. "How about seven tomorrow night?"

"Excellent. Tonight I'll have my own little celebration all by myself. Tomorrow night we'll make wedding plans."

"Are you taking charge of my life?" he asked, looking amused.

"I wouldn't dream of it. You're capable of taking care of yourself."

"I'm glad to hear you think so," he said, smiling at her.

"I'm going in and celebrate."

"Save some celebration for tomorrow night. When I leave here, I'll go see my mom. I want to tell her and my grandfather about you. My grandfather's days are really limited. He's a sick old man."

Marc caught her lightly beneath her chin, making her heart flutter. "You're absolutely sure, Lara? You can take tonight to think—"

She stifled his words with a finger to his lips. "I'm absolutely sure I want to marry you on a temporary basis."

He smiled and she pulled her hand away. "Good. You've made me happy, and you've solved a big dilemma for me. I want to keep Grandpa happy in his last days. I don't want him to worry about his family."

"That's good, Marc. You're a good guy."

"Maybe not quite so good," he said as he shook his head. "I am going to inherit a lot if I do what he wants."

"You could get along without all that. You love the ranch because of your grandfather."

"You keep seeing that halo over my head," he said.

"There are moments it's there. Moments," she said, smiling at him.

He laughed. "That's what I thought from my very practical secretary. You don't really see me as such a saint."

"With what you're going to do for me, oh, yes, I do see a halo. Now, I think you should let me say good-night and go inside."

"Of course," he said, stepping away. "I'll see you tomorrow, and tomorrow night I'll take you to dinner and we'll plan our wedding."

"I can't believe it."

"Start believing. I'm really happy, Lara, and I hope you are, too."

She smiled as she watched him walk toward his car. Only when he pulled away did she go inside.

When she shut the door behind her, she finally let go. Shouting for joy, she spun around her entryway and stopped in front of a mirror that had belonged to her mother. She looked at herself. "Mrs. Marc Medina. Hello, Mrs. Marc Medina," she said, feeling tingles each time she said her future name. She was going to marry him. She would have enough money for her future, for her education, for her baby. More than enough money. She'd even be able to pay some of her mother's medical bills. Marc was being incredibly generous. He was a multi-millionaire, but he must be inheriting a lot to be so generous. She waved her arms in the air and spun around again.

"Mrs. Marc Medina," she repeated, looking at herself again. This time, though, her exuberance was tempered. She told herself she needed to guard her heart well, because Marc would stick with his plan and end their marriage. She knew he was strong-willed and she would be deluding herself if she thought he would fall in love and want to stay married. That wasn't what she wanted, anyway. She wanted to be a doctor and to pursue a career in medical research.

Meanwhile, Lara intended to enjoy Marc, have a good time with him and keep her heart absolutely locked away. She turned to face the mirror again. "Can you do that when he is handsome, fun, and oh, so sexy?"

Yes, she could keep from going to bed with him. She'd known him a year and hadn't slept with him, hadn't fallen in love with him. She didn't want emotional hang-ups tangling up her life now that she could do so many things she'd planned on doing. She had to resist his appeal.

"After this marriage I have plans for my future and Marc Medina is no part of them. And Marc has plans for his future and I'm not part of his plans," she told her reflection in the mirror. "Remember that. I have plans for my future and I can't wait to start."

She rushed to her closet to plan what she would wear to work.

It was past 2:00 a.m. when she fell asleep, and her dreams all included Marc Medina.

To her relief, the next day at work she was too busy to think about her new life or her dinner plans, and she barely saw Marc until after four when he postponed their talk and told her he would pick her up shortly before seven.

After work she rushed home to shower, change clothes and take down her hair, aware it was the first time that she'd have her hair down with him and be dressed in a flirty, flattering outfit. Was he even a fraction as excited as she? She suspected he merely viewed their dinner the same way he would one of his business dinners where he was about to close a deal.

She, on the other hand, could barely contain her excitement or stop thinking about the fantastic fortune he would give her. But along with her excitement came a constant nagging worry that she should guard her heart or risk getting badly hurt. She had to stay out of his bed, because sex would mean nothing to him except physical satisfaction. She had to be on constant guard against seduction that would be briefly satisfying and then could bring down all sorts of problems for her.

She needed to keep a wall between them, she reminded herself. Eventually, they would part and he would never look back. By then if she had her baby, she'd better have her life in order.

As she laid out clothes to wear, she looked at herself in the mirror, studying her stomach, which was still flat. She wasn't far along in her pregnancy and she was tall and slender. Most people would think this baby was Marc's and he was agreeable to that. Why was he being so generous with her? Was it because of the loss of his own baby and his wife? She knew he was relieved to find someone who would be happy to part when he ended their marriage—she could understand that one and how she was probably the only woman he knew who would walk away with a smile. And she'd better maintain that distance from him so she would be able to leave without any kind of hurt. She had worked for him for a year and she could say goodbye and be okay right now. She wanted to feel the same way when they ended their marriage.

When her doorbell rang, she took a deep breath, picked up her purse and went to answer. Her new husband-to-be and her new life stood waiting on the other side of her closed door.

Three

While he waited for Lara to come to the door, Marc looked at the neat flowerbeds bordering the porch of the small house where Lara lived. He wondered how much they would see each other once they wed. She could settle on the ranch because he knew that's what his grandfather wanted. Other than that, he didn't care what she did to get ready for her baby and to go back to school when their marriage ended.

The door swung open and he turned, momentarily startled. "Lara?" His gaze swept over her and his pulse jumped unexpectedly. His eyes narrowed as he stared at her. "You worked until your regular closing time, so you had just an hour to get ready."

"That's right," she said, looking at him with wide, curious blue eyes.

"You look gorgeous."

She smiled. "Thank you. Come in and see where I live."

He walked into her place, not because he was interested in seeing where she lived. He merely wanted to look at her longer.

"You let your hair down. I never see you like this."

"No, this isn't how I want to look at the office. I stick to business there, as you know. We get things done, and that's what I want. Tonight's a little different and it's not an office event. It's a celebration, so I dressed for the occasion."

"Did you ever," he said. "You look absolutely wonderful. I'm happy all over again that I asked you and you accepted." His gaze swept over her again. Her thick, long dark brown hair was brushed back from her face, caught and pinned on the sides of her head to fall freely with the ends in big, loose curls. He had the ridiculous impulse to tangle his fingers in the inviting mass.

"Come in and look around." She turned and he followed her, his gaze slipping over her much more slowly, drifting down to her tiny waist. She had a slight, sexy sway to her hips as she walked. She wore a sleeveless black dress that ended above her knees. It was formfitting, beautiful and seductive with her figure. And she did have a figure, something she hadn't shown to this extent before.

And he had never seen as much of her legs before. Now he discovered her legs were long, so long and shapely that he couldn't stop admiring them. But this new discovery was disturbing. He didn't want to find her highly appealing. He wanted the kind of impersonal relationship they'd had all year at the office. His heart was still locked away, numb after losing Kathy, and he didn't want involvement with Lara, a night in bed with her because of lust and then all kinds of emotional complications. He wanted to stay out of her bed and keep this marriage in name only. But he'd just discovered that was going to be more difficult than he had imagined. He tried to reassure himself by thinking about their past year working closely together. There had never been even one second of flirting, much less anything more.

As he glanced again at her legs, he didn't feel reassured.

Her home was filled with furniture that looked as if she had inherited it from her mother—a big comfortable-looking wooden rocking chair plus two wingback chairs in deep blue upholstery and a matching sofa. He gave his surroundings a cursory glance and returned to looking at her.

"You have a nice place."

She smiled at him as she picked up her purse. "It's plain and small, but adequate for me."

"If you're ready, shall we go?"

"I'm ready," she said, and she locked up as she left.

He couldn't keep from looking at her. "You've never looked like this at the office."

"I think the way I look at the office is more conducive to a business atmosphere and I don't care to draw undo attention to myself."

"I think all that might have worked to my advantage," he said, wondering if this was going to be the purely businesslike arrangement he had anticipated.

He held the door for her, and when she slid into the seat, he glimpsed her gorgeous long legs as her dress slipped high above her knees before she pulled it down slightly.

As he closed the door and walked around the car, he was hot, intensely aware of her and wanting to get another long look at her. And that's when he had his answer. He would never see his secretary quite the same way as he had before this evening. Not after he'd had a glimpse of the good-looking woman she actually was.

At the restaurant they sat in a secluded corner. He ordered a glass of milk for her and white wine for himself, and she laughed when he held up his wine glass. "To a fabulous, brief marriage that will reward us both," he said.

Her eyes sparkled and her full lips curved in a tempting smile as their glasses clinked slightly.

"A glass of milk doesn't have quite the ring that two wine glasses do when touched in a toast," she observed.

"No, it doesn't." They both drank and he set down his glass. "Let's order and then we can talk about a wedding."

After they had given their orders, he reached across to take her soft hand into his. To his amazement he felt sparks from the slight touch. Since when did he feel any electrifying reaction from merely touching a woman's hand—particularly his secretary, whom he saw every day? As he released her hand, he wondered how much she was going to become involved in his life in this brief, fake marriage of convenience.

He hadn't expected he would notice her much more at the ranch than he had at the office, but he had miscalculated where his quiet secretary was concerned. He should have paid closer attention, but he was still pleased with his choice. She would be perfect in so many ways, mainly in moving on when the year was up. Plus, she needed someone and he could help her and her baby. He knew she was locked into that education and career, and neither hell nor high water nor anything he did would change it. He was completely familiar with a woman driven to accomplish something.

"Now, what kind of wedding would you like to have?" he asked. "Remember, it has to be this month."

"I think, given the circumstances that you and I are not in love," she said quietly, her big, blue eyes making his heart race, "I think we should have a small wedding. I'm not far along in my pregnancy and if we have a small wedding this month, by the time I have to announce that I'm pregnant, people will think it's your baby that I'm carrying. Are you all right with that?"

"Yes, I am. That was part of this deal. I told you that your baby can have my name."

"Marc, you're really generous," she said, her eyes shining.

"Just remember, I'm gaining, too."

"Is a small wedding all right with you? Because you have all sorts of people you probably are obligated to ask. I have no idea about your relatives except what you've recently told me."

"My close relatives will be there—my mom, my grandmother. My closest friends, Gabe Callahan and his wife. I'll ask Gabe to be my best man. After the ceremony, we'll have a big reception and invite our friends, everyone we want."

"Since I don't have relatives and you do, if you'd like, we could just have a small wedding at the hospital— then your grandfather could be present. If he's able, we could have it in his room or just outside his room."

"You're willing to do that?" Marc asked, surprised and pleased.

"Yes, because it doesn't matter to me, and I can marry in a week, if you want."

His pulse jumped because he didn't expect this much cooperation from anyone, even her. It was enough that she'd accepted his proposal. "That's fantastic, Lara. The sooner we marry, the sooner the clock starts ticking on the year I have to stay on the ranch. Also, something could happen to my grandfather at any point and I would like for him to know that I married and did what he wanted."

"That's good. We need to get the license."

"I'll take care of that," he said, guessing she was moving back into secretary-boss mode. They paused when the waiter set green salads in front of them, and once they were alone, they continued discussing the wedding.

"We should be able to marry Saturday, if you can, or even Friday," he said, and she nodded.

"Either one is fine. I'd prefer to avoid missing the class I'm enrolled in. I go to Denton to school on Wednesday nights, so Friday or Saturday won't be an interference."

"When we move to the ranch, you'll have a hell of a drive."

"It's only once a week until December. I'll do it," she said, and he knew she would. He gazed at her. She was perfect for this temporary marriage of convenience. She would walk away as easily as he would. For a real marriage, though, she was the type of woman he vowed he would never marry—a driven woman who put business first even though her motives were to help others and work toward a cure for illness. She would work long hours—just like his mother always had. He didn't need her for the real thing, though, so this would work beautifully.

"I expected a lot from this job, but never marriage to the boss. Wow," she said, laughing, her eyes sparkling.

"I'll have my accountant contact you and set up an appointment. You need to open an account where we can deposit funds on a regular basis, so you'll have money available. Before we part tonight, I'll give you a check for the wedding, your dress, that sort of thing."

She laughed again. "I cannot believe this is happening to me."

"It's real and it'll get more real when you're Mrs. Marc Medina."

"Mrs. Marc Medina," she repeated, shaking her head. "Absolutely impossible."

"It's possible and it's happening, and we'll both benefit," he said.

When she turned those wide blue eyes on him, his pulse jumped. Still, he knew if they could resist going to bed together and manage to keep this relationship just like it was tonight—no desire or flirting or wanting each other—then when it came time, parting would be easy. But he suddenly had a feeling it wasn't going to be as easy as he anticipated. His reaction to her had changed, and it shocked him how much restraint he was having to use around her. How could she cause the sexy reactions he was having?

He tamped down those tingles of awareness and focused on the business at hand.

"I didn't talk to my mom or grandfather last night," he said. "I wanted to wait until dinner tonight and see if you had second thoughts. You do understand that when the year is up, we'll divorce, right? I'll have a contract drawn up. I don't want you to have any illusions about staying married."

"I understand and I won't. I'm marrying to pay for my baby and my education, not for romance," she said and then blushed. "Sorry, that sounded very crass."

"No, it didn't. It sounded very honest. So am I. We have the same motives and goals so we understand each other and we'll walk away and never look back."

"I'm thrilled," she said, smiling at him, and his insides clutched. In an instant she could make him hot and wanting her. Where was this physical attraction coming from? That had not happened in the office and she wasn't causing it deliberately now. Was he getting in deeper than he had intended? He brushed that question aside as impossible.

"I've been totally alone and on my own for so long. This is going to be a different world, even a marriage of convenience that is only temporary."

"I guess that's why you're very independent."

"I didn't know it showed," she said.

"A little. It's not bad to be independent," he said.

He thought about how much time they'd be spending together over the coming year. The ranch house was big. Would they naturally drift together or would they gradually drift apart and barely see each other? He hadn't put many stipulations in his proposal, nor could he, really. But in his mind he knew what he had to do. Keep his distance.

He kept telling himself that all through dinner, whenever the urge to take her hand threatened him.

Dinner was pleasant, despite the undercurrent of tension. They talked about the wedding and life on the ranch. Finally, he took her home, walking her to her door.

"Want to come in?" she asked, smiling at him.

He shook his head. There was only one thing he wanted.

He put a hand on the door and leaned down till his mouth was a breath from hers.

He was about to kiss her.

She backed up quickly, resisting the urge to place her hands on his chest and push him away. She didn't need the physical contact.

"We agreed to avoid sex in this union. We might as well stick with that tonight," she said, feeling he was on the verge of changing their relationship. "We both have to remember this marriage of convenience is headed for a divorce in one year. Let's pass on kisses."

He looked amused as he nodded. "That's the smart thing to do." He took a step back. "I'll talk to my family and get back with you about when you can meet them." He looked down into her eyes. "Lara, you're right in that we'll both be better off to leave kisses out of this. You and I want to walk away someday and it'll be a lot easier if we keep this relationship somewhat like what we've had this past year."

"I agree. Now, you may have certain expectations, since I've been your secretary and at your beck and call every work day for almost a year. I think we need to establish right now that that's over."

"Are you going all independent woman on me?"

"I might be. After all, this isn't a boss-secretary relationship we're entering into. We'll have adjustments to make. You'll have adjustments to make, I'm sure, because I won't be your secretary any longer," she said. "What's far more standard now, if I'm your wife, is for me to start giving you some orders."

His smile grew. "Have you ever been hiding yourself. You're a whole different woman," he said, his gaze drifting over her.

"This is a brand-new situation. We're just getting started in our new relationship, and of course, there will be adjustments, but I will not be at your beck and call as I have been."

He looked amused as she leaned closer and patted his arm. "Whatever we say and do, when the time is up, the marriage is over. You want that and I want that and we both should keep that goal in sight."

"You have an agenda that evidently you don't think can include marriage and a husband."

"I think it'll work better without a husband. Mostly, I know you don't want to stay married, either."

"You're right. That's almost enough right there to make me fall in love with you—you have an agenda you'll stick by, a bargain we made that you'll keep, and I can trust you completely to do as you promised. I can't say that about any other woman I know. Don't think you aren't greatly appreciated."

"I can be even more appreciated," she said in a sultry voice, flirting with him. Instantly, she stepped back. "Oh, Marc. I take that last remark back. That's a line I don't want to cross. Let's keep this relationship as much like it has been as possible."

"I agree, Lara. That's the sensible thing to do and it'll be best for both of us in the long run. I have to tell you, though, I'm appreciating you more by the second right now," he said.

"Then I'll just say goodnight," she said. "It was a fun evening and we're moving along."

"This is going to be good for both of us. You'll see. I'm happy with it," he said, meaning what he was saying. "I'll see you tomorrow. It was a fun evening, Lara."

"I had a wonderful time."

"I feel very fortunate to have you for my secretary and to have the wits to propose to you. You're perfect for this and you won't fritter away a lot of the money on clothes and jewelry. And you've agreed that we'll avoid sex, which we easily did this past year."

"I should hope I wouldn't have sex with my boss. As for clothes and jewelry, there is enough money coming that I can get some new duds if I want them," she teased, and he smiled again. Impulsively, he hugged her.

"Wait, let me get a picture to show Mom. I want to tell her about you before I take you to meet her." He held out his phone and took Lara's picture. He then stepped beside her, slipping his arm around her waist to take a picture of the two of them.

"There," he said, showing the pictures to her.

"Will she approve of me?"

"Of course. If I've proposed to you, she'll trust my judgment. We're close. We've always been a close family. I was close with my dad."

"Do you look like your dad?"

He laughed. "Not at all. He was much shorter and had straight black hair. He had brown eyes, too. That's about the only similarity. I look a little like my mom, but she's short. I don't know where I get this height. My grandfathers aren't tall."

"I'm glad you're close with your family. I look forward to meeting your mother. Tell your mom you didn't get me pregnant. She'll think this is your baby and her first grandchild. I don't want her to be upset when the marriage is over in the fall."

"I'll tell her the whole deal. But I'm warning you now. My mom will get attached to your baby. She miscarried several times and she loves babies. No matter what we tell her, she'll treat this baby like her first grandchild for sure."

"She'll always be welcome to come see us. I'll be in the area."

"We don't have to worry about that now. I'll see you tomorrow."

She stepped back and her eyes were wide as she gazed at him. "Dinner was delicious. I had a fun, interesting time and I'll see you tomorrow evening. Thank you for dinner."

"We're off to the best possible start," he said.

"As long as we aren't stirring up trouble."

"No. You have your eye on your agenda and my heart is locked away."

Her expression changed and she looked solemn. "That's right, Marc. I'll see you tomorrow." She opened her door and stepped inside. "Good night," she said.

"Night, Lara." He turned and walked down the steps and headed to his car. In minutes his taillights disappeared around the corner.

It was early in the evening and Marc drove from Dallas to Downly where his mother still lived and had her successful restaurant that drew people from Dallas daily in spite of the distance.

He turned into the house his mother had built when he was in college. By then, the money problems had vanished and her restaurant was a success; his grandfather was a help and Marc was on a scholarship. The one-story house was set back on a landscaped lawn with flowers still blooming in the warm Texas fall.

He had called her and when he circled the white stucco house to the back, she stood in the doorway waiting for him.

Pilar Medina was short with thick black hair and brown eyes, and he loved her and appreciated all she had done for him as he grew up. He hurried to the house, and as soon as he stepped inside, he hugged her and kissed her cheek.

"Come in. Have a drink. We can sit and talk and you can tell me what you're doing."

"How's Grandpa today?"

"He had an easier day and the nurses are so good to him."

"Good. I'll have a beer and I'll get it. What can I get for you?"

She waved her hand. "Nothing, thank you. I'll just listen."

He smiled, knowing she would do more than just listen.

Out of habit, they sat at the kitchen table and she

placed a bowl of pretzels in front of him. She sat and gazed expectantly at Marc.

"I want to do what Grandpa wants. I'll marry this month."

"Marc, I don't know about this pushing you into a marriage. He keeps telling me to stop worrying. He says he knows what he's doing and he says he knows his grandson and what's best for you."

Marc had to laugh as he shook his head. "Sometimes I don't think he realizes I'm a grown man now."

She smiled and patted Marc's hand. "He loves you with all his heart. He's been a good father to me and a good grandfather to you. And he stepped in when we lost your father."

"What Grandpa doesn't know is that when the year is over, I'll end the marriage. I'll have papers drawn up that the woman I will marry will sign, agreeing to my terms."

Pilar rubbed her forehead. "Marc, I still worry. This marriage of convenience—Grandpa should not be forcing you into that."

"I want to make him happy. I want to do what he wants and I want his last days to be happy, without worries about me and you and, above all, about Grandma and the ranch. He wants me there to run the ranch and he knows I'll see to it that she's taken care of and can live in their house where she wants to stay."

"You're a good son and a good grandson, but this worries me."

"Stop worrying. I've already worked it out. I've proposed to someone, Mom."

"Aye, aye, aye. Who is she?"

"The perfect person. She's Lara Seymour, my secretary." He pulled out his phone. "Here's her picture. She has a master's degree and wants to go to medical school. She has no family. The dad walked out years ago. Her sister died when she was young and her mother died just a few years ago and it's because of her mother she wants to study medicine so she can go into medical research to work toward finding cures. I've made her a good offer, enough money to cover her expenses for her education."

"Ah, Marc, I worry about this and I cannot talk your grandfather out of it. He is determined. He tells me he knows what he is doing. How can he know what he is doing when he interferes in your life and he's a sick old man in a hospital bed?"

"Leave him alone. He won't change his mind and I don't want him worrying."

Pilar wiped her eyes. "I worry. I worry about Grandpa and Grandma. I worry about you. I know you love them and are good to them. You're good to me, too."

He smiled. "I love all of you, Mom. Stop worrying. Let me do the worrying," he said gently, hugging her lightly and kissing her temple. "You're worrying for nothing. Lara is going to be perfect for this, and besides, it's a temporary situation."

"Once she legally becomes your wife, she may not want to leave."

"This one will. Lara has been a great secretary. I know she'll cooperate completely." He told her how she'd been engaged and how she'd broken the engagement. "She hasn't told anyone at the office except me, but she's pregnant with his child."

His mother frowned at him and her face paled. "No," she said softly. "Ahh, Marc."

"It's all right. The money I'm giving her will take care of her and her baby. She can afford a nanny. I'll set up a trust so her baby's education will be paid for. I told her this baby will have my name and that's fine with me."

"Marc, this little baby—you won't be able to dissolve this marriage. You're going to love that child."

"This is not a permanent marriage. It's a marriage of convenience and it will end."

"It may end and it may not end. You might fall in love."

"I won't. I promise I won't. I've worked closely with her for a year now and there's nothing between us except I respect her and want to help her. She's a fine person, but we won't fall in love. She has her life planned out. Don't worry," he said, wishing his mother didn't even have to know the details of the arrangement. She looked shaken and unhappy, even more worried than before.

"Oh, Marc," she said, grasping his hand and gazing at him intently.

"Please, don't worry," he said, surprised by how badly she was taking this because she knew the demands on him that her father had made. "Mom, you know how much you wanted the restaurant to succeed. Well, Lara is like that about becoming a doctor. That's all she really wants for herself and her baby. She will leave me when the year is up and she won't change her mind. She's as driven as you are. Her fiancé wanted her to get an abortion, so she broke the engagement. This baby will give her a family."

Pilar's eyes filled with tears that she hastily brushed away. "Marc, I knew this day might come and I finally think it has. You are marrying and it's different from when you married Kathy. I thought about talking to you then, but you were so in love, so happy. I didn't want to do anything to worry you. You are older now and are marrying again. You think it won't last and it probably won't, but I think it is time for you to know some things that I've never told you."

He smiled. "We have dark family secrets? Tell me. I'm sure there's nothing disastrous."

Surprising him, she didn't smile. She caught his hand and held it. "Your father loved you with all his heart and he was a good father to you."

"The best. I loved him, too. He was a very good

dad. And I have a very good mom and very good grandparents. Now, what's worrying you?"

"There is something I haven't ever told you. There is a secret I've never shared with you. Now you're marrying this woman and she's having a baby. It isn't your baby, but it is a reminder that you don't know what your future will be. I think I need to tell you some things."

Startled, he gazed at her, unable to imagine what dark secret his mother could possibly have hidden from him all these years. They had always been a close family and he was at a loss because this was so unlike his mother.

She wiped her eyes. "I was so young when we moved here. So young, so inexperienced. I worked for Gabe's family. I never dreamed you would be best friends."

"We were the same age, went to the same schools growing up and played high school football together. Seemed the natural thing to me."

"I'm glad. I cleaned house for the Callahans and lived in the maid's quarters on the top floor of the mansion. I was only fifteen when I started and my second year there Mrs. Callahan was pregnant with Gabe. By that time my father had gotten a job with the rancher and he and my mother lived on the ranch, so I was on my own. I left the Callahans and got a little place in Downly and started selling my tamales. Then I met your father. We were married the first month we met. He was twenty-two and I loved him with all my heart." To his amazement, his mother covered her eyes with a handkerchief and cried quietly. He knew she was remembering his dad and reached out to squeeze her arm lightly in a sympathetic gesture.

She faced him. "I'm sorry for things I did, but I can't be sorry that I have you. You know how I love you."

"Of course I do. And I love you. What's worrying you, Mom? It can't be that bad."

"Marc, understand that I was very young and on my own. Your father came along and loved me and it was true love for both of us. You are going to marry, and while it is a marriage of convenience, it will change your life. You don't know what tomorrow will bring. I think you need to know what I'm going to tell you. Very few people know the truth because of the time element."

"Mom, just tell me what you're trying to say," he said, smiling at her.

She grasped his hand tightly and her hands were icy. Worry filled her dark eyes and he couldn't imagine what could be so terrible that she was this upset.

"Your bride-to-be—there are some parallels to my life."

"How so?" he asked, staring at her and wondering what she was getting at.

"Marc, I worked for Dirkson Callahan." She closed

her eyes and her voice was soft. "I got pregnant with Dirkson Callahan's baby," she whispered.

Stunned, Marc felt as if he had been punched in the gut. He stared at his mother. There was only one reason she was telling him this. Without thinking, he jumped out of his chair and backed up.

"Dad wasn't my blood father," Marc said.

She shook her head. "I married him so soon afterwards, everyone thought he was. I didn't even tell your grandparents. Grandma and Grandpa to this day don't know the truth. Your dad knew the truth and he truly loved me. We loved each other and he was so good to me. Everyone thought I was pregnant by him. There was never any suspicion or breath of scandal."

"I'm Dirkson Callahan's son," Marc whispered. He shook his head as if realizing where he was and that he was standing. He sat down again. "That's why you quit working for the Callahans. Gabe and I are the same age—Dirkson got you pregnant the same time his wife was pregnant," Marc said without realizing he had spoken the words aloud. He didn't want to think about Dirkson Callahan being his father. "He was a lousy dad for Gabe. For all of his sons. He didn't speak to or recognize Blake Callahan, his illegitimate firstborn. And he's my father," he said, stunned by the revelation. "Gabe and I are half brothers. No wonder we get along."

She sobbed. "I'm sorry, son. But you need to

know. I always knew the day would come when I'd have to tell you the truth."

"Dirkson Callahan knows he's my father, doesn't he?"

"Yes, of course. He gave me money to leave and I agreed to never reveal the truth to anyone, including you. He wouldn't give me the money unless I did and I signed a paper to that effect. I told your dad before I married him, and he said he would be your real father."

"He was. John Medina was my true father in every way except biologically. He was a wonderful father and I loved him and respected him." Marc couldn't stop the next statement. "I think Gabe should know."

"If he does, then word will get out and Dirkson will know I finally broke my promise," she said, looking stricken again and wringing her hands. "He gave me money to start my tamale business on the condition I never tell anyone the truth, including you. He's a powerful man, Marc."

"So am I, Mom. Trust me, I don't want to claim him as my father. I promise you that."

"Will you share this with your future bride?"

"No. I'm not sharing this with anyone. Not even Gabe. I don't want to hurt you. And I don't want to hurt Gabe and his brothers—although I think they're immune to being hurt by their dad any longer."

His mother reached out for his hand. "Your Lara. You and she are in the same situation I faced. You will claim another man's child as your own. How could this happen to you? Grandpa should not have made such demands on you."

"He's doing what he thinks is best for me and for Grandma. He's sick and he's old and I don't think he's thinking clearly on this—wanting me to marry this month."

"I know, I know," she said, while tears spilled down her cheeks.

He put his arm around her and hugged her. "Stop worrying. Dad was my dad. So I have some Callahan blood—I can live with that. I didn't have Dirkson in my life. I had a wonderful dad and John Medina is my real father as far as I'm concerned. And he was a great dad and deeply loved. End of story. This is now our shared secret and that's that. When I tell someone—if I ever do—I'll let you know. A part of me feels Gabe should know, but it might not ever happen. It really won't matter. We're already best friends. Otherwise, there's no one now who needs to know."

"I know you'll do what you think is best. Marc, that paper I signed—if I ever let the truth be known, I have to pay Dirkson back the money he gave me."

"Mom, I can pay back every penny and never miss it. I know it wasn't a gigantic sum because you started your tamale business with nothing except a cart. Oh, damn. That's why you worked so hard. You were trying to earn enough to take care of yourself and me.

You had a tiny little hut. I've seen the pictures. Oh, Mom, I'm proud of you. You did so well. Don't worry one minute about paying Dirkson Callahan back. I'll take care of him, if necessary." Then the realization sank in and he nearly spat out the words. "Damn, I'm a Callahan."

His mother shook her head. "By blood only. Remember that. You're a wonderful son and, like your real father and your grandfather, you're a fine man. They raised you. Think of it like a blood transfusion."

He laughed and shook his head. "I don't think I can quite see it that way."

"I knew the day would come when I would have to tell you."

"You've told me and that's that. Now stop worrying about it. It's still a secret and I love you and Dad as much as I did when I came through the door an hour ago. I'll always think of John Medina as my dad. I barely know Dirkson Callahan."

She smiled at him and patted his cheek. "You're a precious boy."

He grinned. "I love you, Mom. Now, we better get back to the wedding discussion. It's coming up soon. I want to bring Lara by to meet you."

"Let's all have dinner at the restaurant. I'll get Grandma there, and we'll take a plate to your grandfather."

"You know he can't eat tamales and chili. Or he

isn't supposed to. I'll take Lara by to meet him, too. I think you're going to like her."

"If you do, I will," she said, smiling at him.

"I have to get going now. I want to go by the hospital and tell Grandpa, if I can get in to see him and he's awake. Otherwise, I'll go in the morning on the way to work."

She followed him to the door and he turned to hug her. "I love you. You're the best mom in the whole world."

She laughed as she hugged him in return. "And you are the best son," she said. "I love you so much."

He smiled at her and left, but as he drove, he couldn't stop thinking about his mother's secret. Dirkson Callahan was his biological father. He felt like Gabe should know. But what would it hurt if he never knew? He and Gabe would be the same friends either way. And there was no reason to share the news with Lara. She was temporary in his life and it wasn't his child she was carrying. For now, the secret was going no farther than his mother's kitchen.

He was thankful his mother had never told him until now. That he had grown up thinking the father he loved was truly his dad. And he was, as far as Marc was concerned. Blood was the only tie he had to Dirkson Callahan. He'd be happy to have Gabe for a half brother, but he already had him for best friend, so that was good enough.

He thought about Dirkson giving all his attention and efforts to business. Marc had a workaholic blood father on one side and a workaholic mother on the other. He could understand why his mother put work first when he was young. She was only sixteen when he was born. Along with his dad, she was trying to make a living. Growing up, he'd wanted her to be homeroom mother or to come to more of his ball games, but she'd been so busy.

Sometimes he had felt neglected, but looking back now, he realized that he had seen his mother's devotion to her work through the eyes of a child. He never thought about how young she was. Fortunately, John Medina came into their lives. Though he'd never made the income that Grandpa or Mom did, he'd shared the load and made his mother happy.

His mother still worked long hours each day when she didn't need to work at all. She was a micromanager, too. He'd always promised himself he'd never get that way or marry someone who was.

He was marrying Lara. She was as driven as his mother, but now he was grateful she had him to help her so she wouldn't have to worry constantly about money or care for her baby alone.

He thought back to the evening he'd spent with her. He'd had a good time discovering her sense of humor and quick wit. If they continued the same kind of relationship they had at the office, he was confident he made an excellent choice for his temporary wife.

Had he?

Or had he brought a heap of trouble on himself by getting tied up with a woman he found attractive?

Four

A week later, on Saturday morning, Lara had butterflies in her stomach. This was her wedding day. A marriage of convenience wedding day. A temporary marriage that was a business deal, actually.

Whatever she called it, this morning she was marrying Marc Medina. She still hadn't met his grandfather because he hadn't been well enough to have company, but she had met Marc's sweet mother, who looked amazingly young. She'd learned Marc had been born when his mother was sixteen.

Wedding traditions had gone out the window and Marc was picking her up. They were going to marry in his grandfather's hospital room—a very unroman-

tic place and definitely not a beautiful one, but hopefully, it would please his grandfather and Marc was
doing what he could for the man.

When the doorbell rang, her racing pulse jumped
again. Her groom waited at the door. She still couldn't
believe this was happening. Not in her wildest dreams
a year ago would she have been able to guess what
she'd be doing on this date. She glanced down at her
tailored pale-pink silk dress. It was conservative, with
long sleeves and a skirt that fell to midcalf. She wore
matching high-heeled pumps.

She opened the door and her breath caught as she
smiled at Marc. In a charcoal suit, white shirt and
red tie, he looked handsome, successful and self-
assured. And so appealing. She tried to ignore that
last thought.

He smiled, stepping into her house and closing
the door behind him. "You look beautiful," he said,
his gaze sweeping over her again.

"Thank you."

"I'm ready to go."

The sun was bright on the cool, brisk September morning. He took her arm and they left to get
into his black sports car. She was aware of Marc's
every touch, of a constant buzzing excitement when
she was with him, a continual warning to keep that
reserve between them she'd always had at the office. He was more relaxed with her now and she
was going to have to keep up her guard. There was

no love in this marriage and she needed to always remember that.

"I'm a little nervous about meeting your grandparents," she told him when they parked at the hospital.

"So far this has been a good day for my grandfather, and up until five minutes ago, it was clear to go see him. Hopefully it will still be that way when we get upstairs. I'm sorry you couldn't meet them before today."

"Me, too." She put a trembling hand to her belly. "I have butterflies in my stomach."

"You shouldn't," he said quietly. "My grandfather will be happy today. Mom will be Mom, looking at you to see if you're suitable to marry her son."

Lara smiled and he took her arm as they walked down the hospital corridor.

Marc had had a dinner party the night before for the small group of relatives and friends who could attend. Most of them were at the hospital now, gathered in the waiting room on his grandfather's floor.

When they reached the lounge, Lara moved around the room with Marc, greeting Gabe Callahan, who would be best man, and Gabe's new wife, Meg. Lara's single attendant was her friend Patsy Wilson, who'd be stepping into Lara's vacated job.

Lara smiled politely as she greeted Marc's mother, who hugged her lightly.

"You look beautiful." She took Lara's hand. "I pray you and Marc find happiness."

"Thank you. My life will be easier because of your son."

"Family, the heart—these are what's important in life. Keep each other happy when you're together. That's what I tell Marc."

"Thank you," Lara said, smiling at his mother. "He has such a nice family."

"Lara, I'm sorry your mother isn't here to see you today," Pilar said.

"Thank you. I wish she was here," Lara said, thinking it was nice of Marc's mother to make such a comment.

Minutes later, when the minister arrived, Marc quietly got the group into their places in his grandfather's room. He took Lara to his grandfather's bedside. "Grandpa, this is my bride, Lara Seymour. I've told you about her."

"I'm happy to meet you," she said, as she looked at the small, frail, white-haired man whose bony hands lay on his chest. When he gazed at her, she felt as if he was alert and very aware of what was happening.

"Grandpa," Marc said, leaning down. "Do you want us to get married here in your room or would you rather sleep and have us go to the visitor's lounge?"

"You marry here where I can see you," he whispered hoarsely.

With Marc directing, everyone lined up and someone started music playing softly on a phone. The wedding was as surreal to her as everything else about Marc's proposal had been.

Lara glanced up at Marc and saw a muscle flex in his jaw. He seemed highly fond of his grandfather, so this might be a tough event, because it made it painfully obvious how frail the old man was.

Everything was in hushed tones, yet she was aware of Marc's grandmother holding her husband's hand and his eyes focused on Marc as Marc repeated his vows. Marc slipped a gorgeous diamond band on Lara's finger and then, finally, she heard the minister say, "You may kiss the bride."

Marc turned her to face him and she looked into his inscrutable brown eyes. She had no idea what he thought, except this was what he wanted.

He brushed her lips lightly with a fleeting, tender kiss, the faintest caress of his warm lips on hers, a feathery touch, yet she tingled to her toes. For a moment she thought this marriage might not be as easy to manage as they'd both anticipated. She had a definite physical reaction to him. Now that they'd be living together, it might be far more difficult to avoid a physical relationship than she had thought.

As soon as the ceremony was over, Marc walked up to his grandfather, who smiled and took Marc's hand in his shaky grip. "The ranch is yours. Take good care of Grandma. You're a good boy. Be happy, Marc, and may you and Lara have a long and joyous union," he whispered, closing his eyes.

Marc leaned down to kiss his grandfather's cheek, and when he turned to Lara, she saw that he battled tears. She thought of her own loss and could understand. She stepped close to take Marc's other hand and squeeze lightly to reassure him. He smiled at her, and for a moment she felt a closeness with him she hadn't ever felt before. To anyone watching, the gesture would seem a natural one between husband and wife. To her, it was a reminder that she needed to keep her distance. That this marriage would be brief and never hold love.

In the lounge, the others congratulated them and Marc's mother hugged her.

"Welcome to our family," she said, and Lara felt a mixed rush of gratitude for Pilar's easy acceptance while she knew it was only temporary. For an instant she felt a stabbing pang, a fleeting wish that this ceremony was real and she was becoming part of this family that seemed so filled with love for one another.

Would she ever find that for herself? She and her mother had been each other's only family for so long, and now Lara didn't even have her. She thought of the tiny baby she carried and looked at Marc as someone said something to him that made him laugh. She wished this baby was his. Another silly wish that couldn't possibly be.

Marc's mother hugged her again. "Be kind to

Marc," she whispered for Lara's ears only. "He's a good man."

"I will be," Lara said. She couldn't help but find the comment odd, because from what she could see, Marc didn't need anything from anyone. He seemed as self-sufficient and self-confident as a human could be.

She looked over at him as he talked to Gabe Callahan. The two men were almost the same height, and they shared the same dark hair, though Marc's was far curlier.

He turned and their gazes met, and she felt as if sparks danced between them. Once again she heard that voice inside her head telling her to guard her heart with all her being. In spite of all this and how nice he had been to her, she knew absolutely, when the time came, he would dissolve this marriage and walk away without ever looking back. She knew his iron will, and there was no way Marc was going to fall in love so she'd better not, either, unless she wanted another big hurt and loss.

He walked up to her, interrupting her thoughts. "Hey, Mrs. Medina, let's move this party to the country club where we can cut loose and have a blast."

"Sounds good to me," she said and hurried out with him as he waved his hand in the air for the others to follow.

To her surprise, Marc had hired someone to plan the reception. She'd figured he would turn that over to her, but she had to admit it was fun to walk into the big ballroom and be surprised by the flowers and the food.

Before long they was seated at a round table with the Callahan brothers. Marc sat on her right and Gabe's wife Meg was on her left. The woman's dark brown eyes sparkled as she gushed, "I love weddings, and you make a beautiful bride."

"Thank you," Lara answered. "Your husband is Marc's best friend, so I'm glad we'll be friends."

"Me too," Meg replied. "Those two guys know how to have fun. I've known both of them all my life, it seems. The Callahans are a great bunch except for their dad, but he's out of the picture most of the time."

Blake Callahan and his wife Sierra were also at the table. Meg pointed them out. "Sometime you'll get to meet the kids. There's Sierra and Blake's little girl, Emily, and of course Cade has adopted their niece, Amelia."

Lara had heard the story. The brother between Gabe and Cade—Nate, Amelia's daddy—was killed in a car crash along with Lydia, his wife. Because Cade had agreed to be guardian if anything happened, he had taken in Amelia. Since then he and Erin had adopted the child.

Meg laughed. "Come to think of it, we all seem to have girls in this family of men."

As if on cue, Cade Callahan joined them, along

with his wife. Erin greeted Lara warmly. "Now you get to be friends with the entire Callahan clan. And we're glad to have you. We needed another woman in this group," she said, smiling at Lara.

"Everyone has made me feel so welcome," Lara said, aware of Marc's arm still across her shoulders.

"To a beautiful bride and a lucky groom," Blake said, his blue eyes twinkling. He held up his glass of champagne in a toast. "May you have a long and happy marriage." They all touched glasses and everyone sipped their champagne except Lara, who only smiled as she set her glass on the table.

As the Callahans talked to each other, she looked around the table. "You have nice friends," she said to Marc.

"I think so." He reached out and took her hand. "And now I think I should dance with my wife."

Three hours later people were still dancing and singing. She had to admit she'd had fun with Marc, who had shed his suit coat to dance all night. He caught her hand when the number ended.

"We've had pictures, cut the cake, danced with those we should. I'd say let's slip out and head to the ranch."

"I'm ready when you are," she said, her pulse jumping at the idea of leaving with him and starting life as Mrs. Marc Medina, even though love wasn't part of the deal. Now they would be living together in the ranch house and she would have to be on alert constantly. She hoped she could get back that very business-like atmosphere she'd had with him at the office, because she could not end up in his bed.

"You go one direction around the room and I'll go the other," Marc whispered to her. "Otherwise we'll just draw a crowd. I'll meet you outside that last door. Go down the hall and turn right."

"Got it. See you soon," she said.

As she spoke to others and drifted toward a door, she glanced over the room one more time. She'd had a fun, touching, beautiful wedding with loads of friends, yet it really was a meaningless event. She wondered why Marc had had the big blowout for a marriage of convenience that would end after twelve months. Maybe it made the event seem more real for his family. His mother certainly seemed happy.

Lara finally stepped out of the ballroom into the quiet hall. At the moment it was empty, and she hurried to the end where Marc had told her to turn right. Before she could, a hand stretched out and snagged hers, and Marc pulled her around the corner.

"Let's get out of here," he said, taking her hand and hurrying to the stairs. In minutes they slid into his waiting car.

"There's a big decorated limo waiting out front and a few people already hanging around it, I suppose to see us come out and leave. Sorry to disappoint them, but this is easier."

He pulled out onto the street. "Well, so far, so

good. We did it. We got married in front of my grandparents and my mother. Thanks again, Lara. You're
the perfect choice and it all went well. My grandfather was a happy man."

"Marc, he's so frail. I'm sorry because I know
how much you love him."

"I do, but I've made him happy in his last days
and he's made me happy, and we'll manage living
on the ranch this year."

They drove to a private airport where Marc had a
plane waiting and shortly they were airborne, buckled into seats in a luxurious lounge. "I stocked champagne for me and lemonade for you. We can sit back
and relax. The rest of the day will be peace and quiet,
which I'm ready for."

"So now I get to see this ranch I've been hearing
about," she said, thinking more about being there
with Marc. He stretched out his long legs. Locks of
black hair curled on his forehead.

"Know much about ranching?"

"Absolutely zero. I'm a city person. I don't even
know anything about small towns like Downly."

"Since you're pregnant and you've never ridden,
you'll have to stay away from the horses and the
barns."

"Believe me, you don't have to tell me twice," she
said, and they both smiled.

How was she going to resist him? This wasn't like
the office, which was so businesslike and fast paced.

Outside of work, Marc was far more laid-back and relaxed. As she thought about it, he reached up to remove his tie and unbutton his collar.

"That feels better. Got anything you want to undo or take off?" he asked.

"No, I don't." She laughed, but her insides jumped at his innuendo. She scrambled to change the subject. "Once we're on the ranch, am I going to be isolated unless I get back to Dallas?"

"Not at all. You'll have me there," he said, leaning close to touch her hand, a casual touch like he'd done several times today. But as with the ones that came before it, the contact caused a sizzling response up her spine. The prospect of guarding her heart seemed more difficult each time she was with him. But she had to resist him, because they each had plans for their futures and none of those plans included the other. If she told him to stop being so friendly, she thought he would laugh it off and pay no attention. Those slight contacts with him didn't have the same effect on him. She was sure of it.

"At the ranch we can think of some way to pass the time," he told her.

"I've already enrolled in some online courses to keep up with my chemistry," she said. "I'm going for a doctorate in chemistry in case I don't get into medical school."

"Chemistry." He leaned forward, placing his hands on the arms of her chair. "I can show you some chemistry we can study right now in this plane," he said in a husky voice.

"You're flirting with me," she said. "We weren't going to do that. I thought this was going to be mostly a business arrangement."

"Relax a little. We might as well have some fun. Sure, I'm flirting with you. You're a beautiful woman and you're my wife now." His eyes were filled with devilment that made her laugh in spite of knowing that the more she encouraged him, the deeper she might sink into flirting and kissing and seduction—all of which she wanted to avoid as long as possible.

"Don't get too appealing and fun," she warned. "You don't want me falling in love with you and vice versa. We agreed about that."

"Once I get to working and go back to Dallas to take care of business along the way, you'll hardly see me," he said. "For now, this is our wedding day and we might as well party a little." He leaned closer, hemming her in.

"That was a really chaste kiss in the wedding ceremony," he said in a low voice. "We might try again and have a little more excitement today."

Sitting like this, she was skirting trouble and breaking her own rules before they even got to the ranch. She put up a hand between them.

"You know full well that we agreed to avoid a sexual relationship. Kissing might lead there," she said. "I don't want to fall in love with you—or even in bed with you. We agreed on that one."

"But you'll hurt my feelings," he said, smiling at her.

"No, I won't," she answered. Before she could utter another word he closed the last bit of distance and covered her mouth with his. His hands slipped off the arms of her seat to wrap around her and pull her closer.

The minute his mouth covered hers, her heart thudded and she couldn't resist his kiss. She wrapped her arms around his neck and clung to him. When their tongues met, a flame of passion sparked deep within her.

Desire—white hot, too long banked—ignited, and she kissed him in return. His hand slipped down over her breast and even though he caressed her through her clothing, his touches were fiery and made her want to be pressed against him even as she knew she shouldn't. Holding him, kissing him, letting him stroke her was taking them straight to disaster. Common sense cautioned her to stop, but her desire was stronger. Marc was incredibly sexy, more than any other man she had known—a discovery she wished she hadn't made—and she couldn't stop kissing him.

She moaned softly and wound her fingers in the short hair at the back of his neck.

She felt his fingers twist loose the buttons on her dress and then drift lightly across her bare breast, and she gasped with pleasure. In minutes he had the front of her dress open, and his fingers pushed away her lacy bra, caressing her lightly. She closed her eyes as she kissed him while sensations rocked her. She was unaware of what he was doing until he lifted her to his lap.

She opened her eyes. "You've put me in danger. We're flying and I should stay buckled into my seat."

"I'm holding you and I won't let go."

"You can't hold me as tightly as a seatbelt," she whispered between kisses.

"Yes, I can, and this is a smooth, safe ride and you're safe in my arms."

"I'm not safe from falling in love with you," she whispered.

She gasped with pleasure as he caressed her breasts with feathery strokes that made her tingle. With an effort she opened her eyes and wiggled out of his arms.

He looked at her intently. "I want you, Lara."

"That wasn't necessarily going to be part of the deal."

"Whatever we both want and whatever works out is part of the deal. I don't have to be in a rush, but Lara, you can't tell me you didn't like that just now or that you didn't like it when we kissed."

"You know I did," she said, feeling a blush heat her face. "But that doesn't make it the smart thing to do."

He smiled and moved his hands so she could go back to her own seat and buckle up again. She looked up to find him watching her intently. "What?"

"You're a beautiful woman. This has been a good plan and a good day. I did the best I could for my grandparents. My grandfather was happy and that makes me happy. He's been good to me all my life and I want to be good to him. You're perfect for this and I'm thankful you accepted the deal."

"Marc, I've benefitted maybe more than anyone. But I think we need to try to keep to our original agreement and avoid sex."

"I'm sure that's the smart thing to do." He nodded, then added, "Relax, Lara. A few kisses are fun and it's not like we'll fall in love because of them. You know I haven't really desired any woman since my wife. You're pretty safe from a heavy relationship."

She didn't want seduction and she wasn't flying to the ranch to go to bed with him. He had been clear that was not part of the deal and for a minute she wondered if he had changed his mind, but evidently not. She took his advice and relaxed.

"Did you tell your mother I'm pregnant?"

"Yes. You told me I could. Believe me, it will end with her. She doesn't gossip."

"It won't be a secret much longer, anyway. Hopefully long enough that a lot of people think this is your baby. That is the nicest thing of all that you offered."

"We're coming in over the ranch. Come here, I want you to see this. I'll buckle you in with me." She laughed as she sat on his lap and he buckled them both in. He slipped his arm around her waist. "This is beautiful country. Look down there at that river."

She looked at lush greenery with the silvery ribbon of sparkling, splashing clear water running through it, spilling over rocks and tumbling between banks.

"This is a beautiful cattle ranch and I love every inch of it," he said, his voice deepening.

"You may not want to go back to Dallas and the corporate world after a year here."

"No, I'll want to go back. I like business and making money. I like both worlds, but now, while I'm young, I want the corporate life and the competition. Later, I can take the peace and quiet out here, the hard, physical work that has a whole different set of rewards."

She moved back to her seat and buckled up again. "I can see that same view out my window," she remarked.

"Yeah, I know. It was more fun to have you sit in my lap and show it to you and know exactly what you were seeing at the time. We'll be landing at the ranch in a few minutes."

"I'm excited." Then a crazy thought hit her out of the blue. "I didn't bring my recipe books."

"That's good, because I have a cook. You won't have to cook or clean. Someone else will do that. For the first week, while we settle in, the cook won't be there, but there'll be enough frozen and ready meals that we'll just have to heat up. And I can grill burgers and steaks, whatever we want."

"In that case, I may enroll in one more course," she said, sitting back for the rest of the flight.

As soon as they landed, they were picked up in a limo, and in a short time she saw a sprawling, one-story house with a porch running the length of the front. "Marc, it's a beautiful house."

"I agree. It was built by the man who owned the ranch before Grandpa, but Grandpa added to it and changed it, so it's his house now. Actually, with this wedding, I'll inherit the house and it'll be mine. That's hard to realize in some ways. In other ways, I've always felt as if this was my family home."

She felt a bubbling excitement as she climbed the porch steps and started to go inside. Marc caught her wrist. "Hey, wait. Let's do this right," he said and dropped the suitcases he carried. He scooped her up into his arms and unlocked the door, carrying her over the threshold.

With her arms wrapped around his neck, she laughed. "This isn't a real marriage."

"It's all you and I have today, and today it is real. For you it's the first, so let's make it as good as we can."

"I told you you're a nice guy," she said, looking into his eyes. She saw the flicker in the depth of his brown eyes and knew when the moment changed. She felt the hot flash of desire and wanted to be pressed against his hard strength. She wanted to be kissed.

His arms tightened to pull her closer and he bent his head. When his mouth covered hers, she tightened her arms around his neck and kissed him back, spinning off into one of his hot, passionate kisses that set her ablaze. The world narrowed down to Marc and she forgot everything else. His kiss deepened, and her insides knotted. Desire made her hot and aching for him. She clung tightly to him, barely aware when he let her slide down against him and then pulled her up tightly. Her heart pounded and desire shook her while she continued to kiss him. Without noticing what she was doing, she wound her fingers in his hair at the back of his head. Her moan of pleasure was a soft sound barely heard above the pounding of her heart.

This kiss was sexy, demanding her response. She didn't want it to ever end and she clung to him, kissing him in return, wanting more, losing all sense of time and place. Finally, he raised his head slightly and she gazed up into his dark eyes that seemed to consume her. Stunned, she was on fire with wanting him. She ran her hands across his shoulders while she fought the temptation to kiss him again. She gasped for breath as she looked at his mouth only inches from hers.

"That got out of hand," she whispered. "We were

not going to do this. We can't start out this way, Marc. This isn't going to work if we kiss."

He stared at her as if seeing her for the first time. "I think you're right," he said, and his voice sounded gruff. He still had that penetrating stare that made her wonder what he was thinking, but she didn't want to ask.

"We can forget that ever happened."

"Not in my lifetime," he said gruffly, and she was startled by the harsh note in his voice.

"Just try," she said. "This is a beautiful house." She looked around, groping for something to get both their thoughts off kisses.

She walked away from him, gazing at her surroundings and trying to focus on anything besides Marc. Her heart still pounded and she had to fight to keep from turning around and walking back into his arms.

"Marc, this is like a set in a movie." She stood in the entryway of what looked like a luxurious mansion. Dark wood paneling covered the walls of the wide hallway that divided and ran in three directions. Overhead a huge crystal chandelier sparkled in the light from the front windows and open door. Gilt-framed oils of Western scenes hung on the walls, while potted palms and other massive greenery lined the walls between settees and groupings of tables and wing chairs.

"I never thought about where you live or what it's

like," she said aloud without thinking as she stared at the opulence surrounding her. "For the ranch I pictured something like an ordinary house or a large, rustic cabin. This is a palace."

"It's Grandpa's ranch home. At least, it was for a while. When they got older, he and Grandma moved into the guest house. They had it enlarged and renovated first, and they've built on to it through the years. Remember, this home belonged to a rancher before my grandfather, and that man never had children. They said he entertained a lot."

"This looks as if it belongs in the city and not out on a ranch."

"This part is a bit formal, I admit, but the great room where we do most of the living, plus the kitchen and informal dining area are casual and comfy. You'll get a full tour later, but right now let's get you to a bedroom. Most of the staff is off this week, but—"

Her laugh cut him off. "The staff? What am I going to be doing here for a year, other than my own plans of studying and going to my classes?"

"Enjoy life. Enjoy the ranch. My grandmother sewed a lot," he said, grinning. "I had a lot of pajamas as a kid because I was the only grandchild. C'mon. I'll show you my bedroom. Bedrooms are off to the left."

"Well, I don't sew. Thank goodness I'm enrolled in courses and can get some things done." Carrying her purse and laptop, she walked beside him and still was more aware of Marc close beside her than of her surroundings. This was her home as long as she was married to Marc. It was palatial, and she couldn't imagine anyone coming inside in muddy boots and walking through the place.

She thought about being here alone when he was out on the ranch or back in Dallas.

"When you're gone, this will be like being alone in an empty hotel."

He smiled. "No, it won't, but you can go into Dallas with me when I go, if you want. You don't have to stay out here every minute. We're married, Lara. You're not working for me and required to remain on the ranch," he said with amusement.

"I'll remember that," she said.

"I'll show you where I told them to put your things. If you don't like it, you can move. We have plenty of rooms. Today is a lazy day, hanging out here, because my grandfather will get a report about our arrival. After that, he probably won't even inquire because he's gotten what he wanted."

"Suppose I went back to Dallas and stayed. Would he know?"

"Yes, he would, but he wouldn't ask. I think he expects things to work out the way he wants. Mainly, I'm sure he thinks when I get back to work on the ranch, I won't want to leave. I *will* want to leave, though. This isn't the life I want right now. It'll be quiet for you to study, so you should get a lot done, and when you need to get to Dallas for your doctor visits, I'll get you there. One of our cowboys, Randall, is also a driver for my grandparents. If you want to have a chauffeur to Dallas, he'll be available."

"I'll remember," she replied as they headed down the hall.

He paused in front of the door to a sitting room. "This is your suite. But first I want to show you mine." He pointed to an open door at the end of the hall. "If you like your room you'll be next to mine." He led her from the hall into a big, comfortable sitting room with a large flat-screen TV mounted on a wall, a desk, shelves with books and pictures, and a big fireplace.

He took her hand and walked through the sitting room into a huge bedroom with a king-size bed, another desk and more walls of bookshelves. Another flat-screen television filled one wall. The moment his hand closed over hers, he drew her attention away from her surroundings. Her pulse began to race at his nearness and touch. She kept telling herself that after the first few days, they would probably go their separate ways and life would be easier. Now she prayed that was true.

Marc turned to her. "You were great today, Lara. My mom really liked you and, of course, my grandparents did." He reached around her and picked up a small, shiny red sack from his desk. "This is for you. Something from me to you that isn't part of a bargain."

Five

Surprised, she looked up at him. "You've given me the world. You don't need to do another thing."

"It's a token of my thanks for not only accepting this deal and marrying me in what is really a marriage of convenience, but also for being nice to my family. That made today better for my grandparents. It made them happy and it made my mom happy. I know she hopes we'll stay together. Mom wants me married." He paused a second. "Anyway," he said, "this is just a thank-you." He handed her the sack.

"Marc, I stand to gain so much from this. You didn't need to get anything for me. I'm thrilled that you asked me and thrilled to do this."

"Open your present."

She smiled at him and opened the sack, taking out a long, black box. She opened it and gasped at the round diamond pendant on a gold filigree necklace with tiny diamonds scattered on the gold. "This is beautiful. It's lovely," she said, touched that he would get it for her. "I'll treasure it all my life."

"Turn around and I'll put it on you," he said. He removed it from the box and she held up her hair as he fastened the necklace.

She was aware of his warm fingers brushing her nape. She turned to look at him and felt his eyes pulling her in. She could feel her resistance wavering. Being here alone with him was dangerous. "Don't make me fall in love with you, Marc."

"You won't fall in love with me because I gave you a necklace. And don't worry. You won't see me for days at a time here."

She nodded, wondering whether it would work out that way or not. But she had meant what she said, when she asked him to avoid making her fall in love with him. He was doing too many considerate things. Making too many sexy moves. Instigating too many fun moments. It would be good when he was out on the ranch working and she was studying. She needed to keep as busy as possible and stay away from him.

"Thank you, Lara, for marrying me," he said quietly, and she nodded. Once again she felt a pang that this wasn't a real marriage. Then she told herself that was ridiculous. They weren't in love and this was nothing more than a business arrangement.

"I hope we both find happiness, Marc," she said solemnly, and he nodded.

"Now let's look where you'll be living while you're here," he said. He led her back to her suite. It was elegant, luxurious and comfortable, like his, but here the decor was done in burgundy, pink and white.

"This is beautiful," she said, thinking her entire house would fit into her suite.

"We'll stroll through the place and I'll give you a tour unless you get tired."

"No, I want to know where things are," she said.

He draped his arm across her shoulders and they left to walk down the hall and look at other suites. "There's an entertainment center on this floor," he said, pointing to an open door. "There's another entertainment center in the wing with the gym."

She wondered if he was even aware of his arm around her. She was, but he talked about his friends and about the ranch and didn't seem to notice. Except he had never done anything like that at the office, so she was certain he was aware of what he was doing.

She thought of the gorgeous diamond necklace she wore, something he hadn't needed to do at all. If he kept up gestures like that, she would fall in love with him, for sure. She shook her head as if to banish the thought and then realized he was prattling on about cattle.

Two wings led off the central part of the house. They walked down the central hall and she saw a huge dining room with a table that would easily seat twenty. Too bad they wouldn't be doing much entertaining in the next year. Not when he viewed their marriage as purely a business arrangement.

She reminded herself to do the same. But Marc was too sexy, too appealing, and now that they had kissed, his appeal had compounded and was far stronger than at the office. She needed to stay so busy she couldn't think about him. If she hardly saw him, he wouldn't care at all. She was a means to an end for him and nothing more. He'd have no struggle in trying to resist falling in love. He knew what he wanted and he had that goal in sight and the rest didn't matter.

Now she just needed to do the same. As if it was that easy.

She followed him into the adjoining room. The kitchen was big, with state-of-the-art equipment. It opened onto a great room that ran across the entire back of the house. A huge stone fireplace dominated the room that also held comfortable furniture placed around a large flat-screen television, and a large desk with two computers and four screens. A pool table stood on one side of the room and a gaming table on the other.

"You have everything in here," she said as she walked around. The back wall was all glass and gave a panoramic view of the landscaped backyard, the patio and the swimming pool with a fountain and a waterfall. "It's impossible for me to imagine your frail grandparents living in this big house."

"Well, they did, and they seemed to fill it. I was here a lot. They've gotten frail now, but they weren't when I was growing up. I visited them at the ranch a lot. Grandpa inherited it when I was seven and I spent lots of time with them all the years I was growing up. Still want to see the rest of the place?"

"Yes, it's fascinating."

"Shucks, I thought maybe you liked my company."

"I wasn't going to tell you," she said and they both laughed.

"Bedroom, great room, kitchen—you're good to go, but I'll show you the other wing of the house. It has a big office for me and I do have it set up so I can work from here and keep in touch with the office while we're living here."

"So, you're not completely letting go during this time."

He shook his head. "No, I'm not. I don't want to turn everything over to someone else and let them run my business. I'll manage it from here. If it works out, I'll go to Dallas for a couple of days every other week. That way I won't lose touch. If you want to go with me, you're welcome to join me or you can go in the limo."

"Thanks. I probably will go to Dallas," she said,

jumping at the chance to be back in the city. "I need to fix up a room for a nursery and this will give me a chance to shop."

"Are you going to live in the same house when this is over?"

"Sure. I just rent, but it's convenient and I know my neighbors and have friends."

"Lara, I'll bet you're married in no time," he said.

She gave him a puzzled look. "Why would you make that statement?"

"You're a beautiful and smart, very capable woman."

"Thank you. That's nice to hear. But remember, I'll have a new baby in seven more months."

"You're the most unpregnant-looking woman I've known. And it's great you feel so well."

"I think it's my height that keeps my stomach flat," she said, placing her hand on it.

"Whatever it is, you don't look or act pregnant."

"I promise you, I am. You can call my doctor."

"Oh, I believe you. You wouldn't make that up."

"No. Marc, I'm so thrilled to be having a baby. This wasn't what I planned, but I just feel like I'll finally have a family again."

He smiled at her. "I'm glad. As long as we're married, you've got a big family because you're part of mine."

"Which I love. Your mother is so nice to me."

"That's because she wants me to marry and settle and give her grandkids. She had me when she was sixteen, so she thinks I'm getting really old to be without a family."

Lara had to laugh and he smiled. "Sometimes I wonder if she was in cahoots with Grandpa on this stipulation to get me married, but then I remember that she stood to lose too much for her to be part of it." They came to another room and he opened the door. "Well, here's my gym."

She looked in on the large gym, then another big office and a sitting room.

"Now you've had the grand tour unless you want to see another office, a ballroom and an indoor tennis court."

"I think I'll unpack and put away my things."

"Sure," he said and once more draped his arm across her shoulders as they walked back to the bedrooms and she turned to enter hers.

"Change to jeans and, later, I'll drive you around the ranch."

"I really should study."

"Maybe you really should, but you can put it off until tomorrow when I'm gone. Besides, you'll be happier if you know your way around here."

"Jeans it is," she said, looking at her suitcases and boxes that had already been put in the suite. When he left, she closed the door behind him and turned to change, but she couldn't stop her errant thoughts. Instead of the upcoming tour, all she could think about was kissing him, no matter how hard she tried to avoid it. She picked up her laptop, as if to remind herself that she had chemistry courses to focus on. She hoped they kept her busy because she didn't want time on her hands and she certainly didn't want time to be with Marc. This marriage was for him to get his inheritance and that was all. She had to keep distance between them and concentrate on her own goals.

She changed to jeans and an aqua sweater, and braided her hair, letting it hang down her back.

She left to find Marc so they could go look at the ranch. When she couldn't find him, she sat in the great room that ran across most of the back of the house.

She heard his boot heels on the wood floor and knew he was coming. Then he swept into the room, and once again, she realized she would be challenged far more than she had expected to keep from falling in love with her new husband in this marriage of convenience.

In boots and a Western shirt, Marc looked even more sexy and appealing than in his wedding suit. His big smile just added to his attraction.

"Ready? We'll drive over some of the ranch. Don't worry, I won't begin to show you all of it and you wouldn't want me to."

She walked out beside him, listening to him talk about the ranch and what his grandfather did to change and update it, but she was far more aware of Marc as he drove the pickup and talked. After an hour of looking at herds of cattle, a corral with horses, a field of bales of hay, windmills and water troughs, she was ready to go back to the house.

"I can find my way in here," she said as they walked in the back door, "but I can't find anything out there on the ranch. I would be lost."

"I've grown up looking at landmarks. I feel like I know the land as well as I know the house. Always keep your phone with you. If you get lost, call me and I'll come get you. Now let's stir up some grub."

She laughed. "I don't think you'll even have to stir. We're stocked until next year."

In a short time he cooked burgers. They sat on the patio in the cool and ate and listened to the waterfall and the tumbling water of the fountain.

Finally she stood, picking up her dishes to carry them inside. "It's been an interesting, memorable day. I'm turning in. I should study."

He stood. "I'll go, too. I'm going to Dallas one day this week. You can go along if you want."

"Thanks, but I think I'll pass this time. I have plenty of studying to do."

"Chasing your dream, huh? I picked the right woman for this marriage," he said.

They walked down the hall together, and at her door she stepped away. "Goodnight, Marc. Thank you for the marriage and for my beautiful ring and for my gorgeous necklace. You did way more than we agreed on."

"I did what I wanted to do. You helped me make my grandparents happy. That's important. You made this deal possible and I didn't know one other woman I could ask. I was really in a bind."

She smiled. "Glad to oblige, though I really think you could have found a few takers."

"And worried every day how I would get rid of them later," he said, shaking his head. "You'll be gone in a flash, off to do your own thing."

"Yes, I will. I'm thrilled that you're enabling me to do that." She slipped into her room. "See you in the morning." She closed the door before he reached out to kiss her. He hadn't stopped her and he might not have reached for her if she had stood there longer, but this way was better. She needed to get on track for her own goals.

She sat down on her bed to study, amazed by her new life and the prospects she had for her future and her baby's future. If she had a boy, she wondered if Marc would like for her to name him Marc. He had been so good to her and that was a good, strong name. There wouldn't be a mix-up later because she and her son would be on their own. Lara Medina. That amazed her. And now her baby would have the Medina name, too.

Later, when she lay in the dark, she thought about her baby and Marc and his name. He would let people think this was his baby. That was the most generous of all the nice things he had done for her. He would claim her baby as his. It would give her baby a father—at least while they were together. It would give her baby legitimacy. Somehow, she was reluctant to reveal the true birth father because he didn't even want his child to live. Marc, on the other hand, had made her child's future bright, with enough money to cover his or her education.

Yes, Marc Medina was a good man. And sexy. And downright dangerous....

That was her last thought before she drifted to sleep.

Marc was seated in the kitchen when she entered the room the next morning. He came to his feet instantly. "You're up early."

"I thought you might be gone," she said, her heart missing a beat as she looked at him. He wore jeans, a navy long-sleeved Western shirt and black boots. He looked incredibly handsome.

"Good morning," he said, his gaze sweeping over her as he walked to her, wrapped his arms around her and kissed her. For one startled moment, she grabbed his shoulders because she felt as if she would fall, but he held her firmly. Then her arms went around him and she kissed him back and forgot to wonder why he kissed her. She was too consumed by the kiss that made her heart race.

When he finally let her go, he smiled down at her.

"I thought we should at least kiss this morning. After all, we're newlyweds."

She placed her hand on her hip and looked at him. "I thought we weren't going to have that kind of relationship," she said, her heart still racing. She tingled and was aware of his gaze drifting over her. How was she going to avoid seduction if this was the way he started each day?

Instead of answering her, Marc swept his gaze from her sneakers and jeans up to her sweater. "I have to say, you look damn good in those jeans. You should have worn them to the office."

"Marc, you're not paying attention to anything I just said."

His eyes finally met hers. "You're serious, aren't you?"

"Yes, I'm serious. I don't want end up in bed. We discussed this and we both agreed to keep it like we had at the office."

"Okay. I can go back to our office hands-off relationship. I was just having some fun. I really didn't mean anything by it and didn't think it would have any kind of lasting effect."

"One kiss now and then might not, but it's still better to keep distance between us and that's what we agreed on. I can't have too big a say in this, I know, because you're the one who made me such a wonderful deal—"

"Stop right there. If you don't want me to kiss

you—even just in fun—you got a deal. We worked together for a year without any kind of physical contact and it was mutually beneficial. We'll go right back to that. I can live with that."

"Thanks. I may hate myself in an hour, but I think that's the smart thing to do."

"You let me know if you change your mind. Or if I get carried away and start to kiss you, just remind me again."

She smiled. "Thanks. I'm trying to see to it that I'll happily say goodbye to you at the year's end."

He walked away to pour a cup of coffee and she wondered if she was going to be filled with regret and longing the rest of the day. The solace was knowing that she had done the smart thing and stopped his casual kisses.

He ate breakfast with her, and then he was gone and the house seemed silent. She realized when he was around it wasn't very quiet, which surprised her because his office had usually been a quiet place. Maybe it was partly the sound of the cowboy boots on the hardwood and terrazzo floors. She had the house to herself until he returned, which would probably be sundown. She suspected he was trying to keep his distance as much as she had tried last night.

She spent the day unpacking and got into the first of her courses. Soon she was immersed in studying, a relief, in that it took her mind off Marc most of the time.

SARA ORWIG 119

She ate early and left him a note that she was studying. She escaped to her suite and closed the door, knowing she was running from spending the evening with him, but that was the sensible thing to do. He'd promised to maintain a professional demeanor around her, but she wasn't one to tempt fate.

They managed to avoid each other for the next two days. He was up and gone before she was out of bed, and at night she ate an early dinner alone and then went to her suite. He had been right in saying there was enough food cooked and ready that they wouldn't have to prepare anything. Without any household demands on her time, she got her course work done quickly and efficiently, which pleased her. She missed seeing Marc because he was fun, but it was better to simply back off and avoid him.

Friday night she was in the kitchen to get dinner when she heard a car. She looked out the window and saw Marc's pickup stop at the gate.

Instantly, she was aware of herself in cutoffs and a blue T-shirt with her hair falling around her face. She shook it back and tried to smooth it down with her hand while her heartbeat raced as she watched Marc get out of his pickup and head for the back door in long, fast strides. She wondered if something had happened.

He opened the door. "Hi, darlin', your husband is home." She had to laugh as he swept into the room with a huge grin on his face. "Get your—" He stopped as his gaze swept her from head to toe, making her tingle.

"My, oh, my, you kept your talents hidden at the office," he said.

She laughed as he looked at her legs. "I don't believe this is appropriate office attire."

"This is one boss it would have pleased," he said.

"I think when you came through the door you were saying for me to get something. Right?"

He finally lifted his gaze and blinked. "Hey, as much as I hate to tell you to cover up a pair of million-dollar legs, get your party jeans. We're going two-stepping. Gabe and Meg are coming, and some guys from the ranch, and we're going to party. I told them we'd meet them in two hours at a honky-tonk in Downly. It's a long drive for us, so that's why the two hours. As soon as you're ready, we'll go."

"Give me a few minutes." Luckily, she'd showered earlier, so all she had to do was change and fix her hair.

"See you here when you're ready. The guys from the ranch are already on their way and they're party animals. Most of them are young and single, but they'll leave the boss's wife alone. And they're a great bunch of guys."

She barely heard him as she ran to change. Twenty minutes later she dashed from her room to find him waiting in the hall. Her heart missed a beat as her gaze ran over him. He wore tight jeans, a black Western shirt, his black Stetson and black boots. Excitement slithered down her spine and she smiled as he straightened up and his gaze ran appreciatively over her.

"You do look great," he said and she smiled.

"Thank you," she said, glancing down at her new boots, jeans and her red Western shirt. Her hair was loose, hanging on both sides of her face and combed straight, although she knew a slight natural curl would make it wavy before the night was over.

"I'm ready."

"Let's go party," he said, taking her arm and hurrying out to his waiting pickup. In minutes they were on the highway. Darkness had set in and she wondered about the evening.

"There's not a person in the world who will know you're pregnant," he said. "You don't show at all. Are you sure you're expecting?"

She smiled at him. "You can stop asking. I'm sure. I'm pregnant, but I don't feel any different yet and I don't think I look different, either."

"I can't believe the doctor has it right. You really don't look it."

"Time will tell," she said, amused that he doubted her.

"You'll have a good time tonight. This is a fun bunch. I've known Gabe and Meg for years, and the guys I work with know how to cut loose and party."

"I can be your designated driver."

"I did better than that. I got us booked into a hotel for the night. Everybody will be staying." He glanced at her as she stared at him and he grinned. "Don't panic. You'll have your very own private room."

She shook her head. "You surprised me there. Thank you. That was a wise decision to get me my own room."

"I'm really good company."

She laughed. "I have to agree on that one."

"I might be better company in the bedroom than anywhere else, for all you know."

"We're not going to find out tonight," she said, laughing at him. "I think you're ready for a party. Are you sure you haven't already had a sip?"

"Me? No. I've been working. I'm just ready for tonight. And I'm tired of cowboys, cattle, bales of hay and my own company. I want to hear someone with a voice higher than mine and dance with my new bride."

"Well, I can accommodate that," she said, enjoying his company after making sure she hadn't seen him for the past week.

"What do you want to drink tonight? I might as well find out now while we can discuss it."

"Think there's any chance of lemonade? If not, I'll take water. If not water, then maybe apple juice."

"I'm sure I'll find something you'll like and can drink," he said.

By the time they parked in the dusty lot in front

of Buster's Beer and Bar-B-Q, the place was packed.
Red neon flickered over the parking lot and music
floated from the building. Marc took her hand and
they entered a big open room with a large dance floor
and a stage. Low lights illuminated the inside. Some
people played pool near the front. On the dance floor,
couples doing the two-step circled the room. Marc
waved at someone as he made his way through the
crowd. He kept his arm around her waist and held her
close against his side. It was easy to put her other arm
around his waist, and she thought that would make
them look like a happily married couple to anyone
who saw them.

She met the men he worked with, greeted Meg
and Gabe, and then Marc took her hand to go to the
dance floor.

It was fun to get out there with him, to dance and
move around the floor in time to the music. Marc
turned her so she danced backward and when he
smiled at her, her heart skipped a beat. It was exciting being with him, even just dancing in a big circle
and not talking to each other at all.

He was the best-looking guy in the place. She realized he was even more handsome and appealing to
her now than he had been in the office. Then again,
she knew him better now. She'd been with him when
he was teasing her, having fun, just being friendly
and kissing her soundly. Her views of him were
changing—had already changed from the days she

was his secretary. He meant more to her now. And tonight would move them even closer together, make them closer friends, make him more appealing and make her want his kisses. It would be a night of fun and excitement, as well as temptation and worries.

She felt the warnings and was aware she hadn't even spent a full week on the ranch with him yet, but she didn't heed them. Not tonight. Tonight she was just going to have a good time.

As they danced in a big circle, she faced him and he smiled at her. His hat was squarely on his head and he looked like the other cowboys in the room.

She was having a wonderful time and wondered how she would fare by the time they finally parted at her suite door. She suspected some kisses at the end of the evening were inevitable. She just needed to remember to stop with kisses.

His appeal heightened as they danced. He was filled with energy and his enthusiasm was contagious. There was no way to resist his appeal tonight. Marc made her feel as if he cared about her and as if this was the best fun ever. At the moment, it was, and she laughed as she danced with him. Once he pulled her close as he spun her around.

"If you think this is fun, just wait until later," he whispered, causing tingles to tickle her insides. He had always looked handsome and confident in his business suits at the office. Now, dressed like the rancher he was, he was sexy, hot and irresistible.

He was filled with vitality and she wanted to stay in his arms.

She had to resist him later, but not now. Now she could dance and laugh with him and work off some of the blazing desire that consumed her.

Enjoy dancing with him, she told herself as he spun her around again. *Just don't go to bed with him.*

In one year he would end the marriage as promised and she didn't want a broken heart when he did. She wanted to be able to walk away as easily as he would. To do that, she needed to stay out of his bed.

She had no idea what time it was when Gabe and Meg told everyone good-night and left. "Should we be going?" she asked Marc.

"Do you want to?"

"Not if you don't. Dancing is fun and I haven't done any in a long time," she answered.

"Gabe and Meg are newlyweds. They want to be off to themselves. These guys we're with will party all night."

"I'm not for all night. Just another hour."

"Sounds good to me," he said. "Let's dance." He took her hand and moved to the dance floor to waltz around the room with her. Their feet flew and she loved dancing. As she enjoyed herself, she realized they danced together as if they had been doing so for years. He was easy to follow and she loved moving to the music, waltzing around the big ballroom and having a wonderful time in Marc's arms.

Finally, over an hour later, he took her hand and leaned close. "Ready to go?"

"Yes, I am," she said, standing when he did. They said goodbyes and waved, and finally left, stepping into the cool night air. The cars had thinned in the parking lot, but there was still a crowd. Marc walked with his arm around her waist and she had hers around him.

"That was so much fun," she said, still thinking about dancing. "We do well together."

"We're perfect together," he stated, stopping beside his pickup. "We have about four blocks to the hotel. We can walk and come back for my pickup tomorrow, if you want."

"The hotel? I don't think so."

"Wait a minute," he said, laughing. "You can have your very own room and I'll have mine if that's what you want."

"It would be, but these are the only clothes I have with me."

"I covered that, too. I have a few things in my pickup and you can get through the night if you can wear the same clothes home in the morning."

Laughing, she shook her head. "I assume you have stuff in that box in your pickup. Walk to the hotel it is."

"Good." He turned to rummage in the back of his pickup and handed her a small backpack and got one for himself. "How's that?"

"It works," she said, glad to walk to their hotel, since it was a nice night and she could use the fresh air. "I'm glad you asked me tonight," she said.

"Yeah. We needed an evening out. How're the courses coming?"

"I'm doing way better than I expected, and faster. That's really all I have to do right now."

"I talked to my mom today. My grandpa wants to come home to the ranch. They can't do anything more for him at the hospital, so we can either move him to a skilled nursing facility or to the ranch. He wants to come here and I can get it set up so he can have home health care and be fine. It'll move Grandma home, too, of course, and that would be good for both of them. I know he'd be happier here, so that's what I'm going to do. I just wanted you to know."

"This is his home," she replied with a nod. "Will that change anything as far as we're concerned?"

"Not at all. They'll be in their house and the only time we'll see them is if we go there," he explained. "I'll have someone to take care of Grandma, too. She just needs someone to help her with little things."

"That's good, Marc."

"I'll go see them, but it won't involve you."

"Take me with you sometimes. Your grandfather wanted this marriage, so it should make him happy to see me. He thinks I'm in your life forever."

He smiled down at her. "That's nice, Lara."

"Tonight was fun. I haven't danced like that in a long time."

"I haven't either when I stop and think about it."

"You work hard. You've told me how hard your mom works. Well, you do, too. You know, I think this year will be a break from all the traveling you've had to do. You fly to look at leases, at wells you have, to corporate meetings with companies where you plan to buy land or rights from them. This is a whole different way of life. I'm sure it's hard, physical work, very different from what you've been doing. And now you're home nights."

"I like that corporate world and I don't mind the travel. I'm not that locked into being home nights."

She laughed. "I'm glad we don't have a real marriage, then."

He grinned and hugged her. "If you were in my bed every night, I wouldn't want to leave the ranch. I wouldn't want to leave the bedroom."

"Yes, well, enough about that."

Luckily they reached the hotel then, calling a halt to that line of conversation. It was a new, three-story building, part of a national chain with well-lit, landscaped grounds.

"Our rooms are the penthouse suite."

She laughed. "The penthouse suite on the third floor."

"Actually, there is a small fourth floor and they do

call it the penthouse suite. As I said, you have your own room—in our penthouse suite."

"So we share the suite, but I have my own room. I can live with that."

He wiped his brow in an exaggerated gesture. "That was easier than I thought it would be. Maybe I should have tried sharing a room tonight."

"That wouldn't have worked," she told him, wagging a finger.

He laughed. "It was a thought."

She waited while he checked in and then he took her arm and they went to their suite. When she walked inside, he closed the door, shed the backpack, just as she had. He tossed his hat on the sofa and crossed the room to her. She turned around to say something to him and forgot what she intended to say when she looked into his eyes. She couldn't get her breath. She was torn between what she should do, what she wanted to do and what he could coax her into doing. Was she going to blow all her resolutions the first night out with him?

Six

He slipped his arms around her and pulled her to him as he leaned down. "I've been waiting to do this all evening long," he said and kissed her.

The minute his mouth covered hers, her heart slammed against her ribs and she was breathless. She couldn't say no or step away. They had constantly touched while dancing, constantly been with each other. But this was different. She was in his arms and she wanted his kisses.

She clung to him tightly as he held her close and leaned over her, kissing her hard and making her pulse race.

His hand ran down her back and over her bottom,

and she moaned softly. She thrust her hips against him. There was no denying she wanted him now. How was she going to resist his kisses? Did she really want to resist?

One night with her husband—would that be a disaster?

She wound her fingers in his thick hair, feeling the short locks curl around her fingers. When his hand slipped beneath her shirt to caress her breast, she gasped with pleasure.

"Marc," she whispered, knowing she should stop him, yet wanting his hands and his mouth on her. She wanted to hold and kiss him and wanted him to touch and kiss her. Temptation and desire had built all evening, if she was honest. Sure, she'd had fun, an exciting time, and his appeal had increased with each hour of dancing and touching each other and laughing together. When had she had that much fun with a man? Not ever. Marc was more fun than any other man she had known. That thought scared her. She didn't want to find Marc anything more than any other man. He would go out of her life later, so she needed to show some restraint.

He kissed her again and then all thought was gone. She was consumed by him. Marc's passionate kisses shut the world away and all she could think about was holding him and kissing him. He ran his thumb lightly over her nipple, tightening it into a taut peak. She loved the feel of it, but it wasn't enough for him, because in seconds he tugged her blouse out of her jeans and twisted free the buttons, opening her blouse while never removing his lips from hers. Each caress, each touch built her need, until longing had her trembling.

Moaning softly, she slid her hands across his broad shoulders. She could feel his erection pressing against her. She knew she should stop. She had promised herself she would use restraint and do what she could to avoid seduction. She hadn't been here a week yet, and she was in his arms, letting him fondle her breast. This wasn't the way to guard against heartbreak. The warning was dim, a whisper to her conscience, and she ignored it momentarily. She wanted just a few minutes more in his arms. All evening she had wanted his kiss, wanted to be in his arms. She couldn't stop this yet.

She leaned away to pull his shirt free of his jeans, just as he had done her blouse. In minutes she had his shirt unbuttoned and she ran her hand over his bare chest while they continued to kiss. His hard muscles did not surprise her because she knew he went to the gym every lunch hour he was in the office. Her fingers tangled in the fine curls before they slid to his flat belly and lower. Her foray was stopped when he pushed aside her bra and leaned down to take her nipple into his mouth, his tongue stroking her, hot and wet, a torment that made her want more.

She gasped with pleasure while she clutched his

shoulders. Her eyes were closed and she was captured by sensation, captivated by his mouth and his hands moving so lightly on her, yet setting her ablaze with longing.

"Marc," she whispered. She knew she should stop, knew every kiss, every touch was bringing trouble, heading her toward seduction.

He shoved her blouse off her shoulders and unfastened her bra, pushing it aside so he could cup her breasts and kiss her. "You're beautiful," he whispered. "So beautiful." His hungry gaze made her tremble and want his hands and mouth all over her.

She gasped when he bent to pick her up and carry her to a bedroom.

When he set her on her feet, she caught his arms to steady herself. Then she looked up at him. "You're going too fast for me."

"We're married, Lara," he whispered. "And I want you."

"It's still too fast, Marc. We're married in a marriage of convenience. There isn't a shred of love and that's a gigantic difference for me. This is pure sex without any love. I need to slow down. We talked about each of us wanting to avoid falling in love. Well, I'm sure you're impervious and could sleep all year with me and still walk away at the end of the year. But going to bed and making love with someone is emotional for me. I can't do that all year and then walk away. I'll be in love," she said, emphasizing *in love* and hoped that would cool him. "We've kissed and we've had a fun evening. Let's call it a night."

He stroked locks of hair away from her face, and she saw the battle play out in his eyes, desire at war with common sense. Then, finally, he brushed a kiss on her cheek and let her go. "Okay. It's a deal," he said. "It still was the best evening I've had in a long, long time."

She smiled at him. "That's the best possible thing you could say. I'm so glad. It was a fantastic evening for me and I had a wonderful time, you sexy man. I couldn't wait to come back and kiss you. You're very exciting, my convenient husband."

"Damn, you send a mixed message."

"You got my message and I appreciate your co-operation. I hope we get to do that again sometime. Just go a little slower so I can deal with my emotions. I'm trying to stop myself from crawling into your bed and wanting to stay. That would mean getting hurt badly when we part."

He nodded his understanding, but he didn't move away. He stood watching her as she pulled her blouse back into place and blushed as she fastened the middle button.

"That'll do for now," she said, picked up her backpack and walked with him across the hall into another large bedroom. While he switched on the lights, she dropped her things on a chair.

"Here you are. I hope you sleep well." She turned to look at him and once again was caught in thickly lashed eyes that conveyed so much desire, she was riveted. All she could think about was kissing him again.

"Aw, hell," he whispered as he grabbed her and kissed her passionately. Finally, he released her and stepped back. She opened her eyes to find him watching her.

"Marc—"

He put a finger to her lips to silence her. "It was a good night and we'll do it again. And sometime, maybe sooner than you think, you won't tell me to go away. But for now, good night." After a few steps he turned back. "If you want anything, or if you want me, just call."

She laughed and shook her head. "Thank you. Don't lay awake waiting for my call," she said.

He grinned and left, closing the door behind him. As he walked away, he wiped sweat off his brow. She made him hot enough to melt. He was surprised by the fun he'd had with her tonight and for the last hour they were there, all he could think about was coming back and kissing her and making love to her. But that wasn't going to happen. Not tonight. But it wouldn't be long, because she couldn't resist kissing him. Meanwhile, he feared he'd get little sleep this night.

He'd had a fun evening—far more than he had expected. When he decided to go to the bar, he'd known the guys would be fun. He hadn't expected much from his city-bred secretary, but he'd thought she might like to get out. How she had surprised him. She could dance and she was exciting, bouncing with eagerness, her big, blue eyes sparkling. He'd wanted to take her back to the hotel, to his bed, make love, hold and kiss her all night long. And the realization shocked him.

He had been numb to women since he lost Kathy. Well, Lara was bringing him out of mourning. He hadn't wanted to dance, to kiss, to take anyone out since he had lost his wife—his real wife, whom he loved with all his heart. He felt as if he had been wrapped in grief for the past fourteen months, but tonight he'd been able to shake off some of the numbness. And he knew Kathy would want him to. She wouldn't want him to go through life dulled by pain and grieving for his losses. She had been filled with a love of life and she would want him to live again. It was just surprising that it was Lara who had vanquished some of that terrible numbness in his life.

Still, he wasn't ready to fall in love. He couldn't, wouldn't. And he didn't want Lara to fall in love, either. He didn't want to hurt her when they parted.

I'm trying to stop myself from crawling into bed and wanting to stay.

He recalled her words.

They had kissed more tonight than he had expected she would let him. At the same time, he also knew that wasn't what she really wanted. She was guarding her heart and she had requested no sex—and he had agreed. He couldn't go back on his promise. He needed to resist temptation and keep this relationship in the friend zone. Could he be a good guy and an honorable man, and keep his word?

Wednesday night Lara drove to Denton to go to class—an hour and a half each way. Despite the distance, Marc was sure she wouldn't miss one class. She'd be a good doctor, that was certain. She was smart, determined, caring.

He missed her tonight. Alone in the house, he grabbed a beer and went outside to the balcony off his suite. He lay back on a chaise, looking at the stars and thinking.

There was much about Lara that reminded him of his mother. Her drive and determination, for example. And he appreciated it, because, like his mother, she had gone above and beyond for him, too, starting with suggesting they marry in his grandfather's hospital room. Very few women would have done that and Marc would always be grateful to her.

And she'd bowled over his mother, too.

He thought of Pilar Medina and was grateful for her sacrifices, as well. Now that he knew Dirkson Callahan was his blood father, he could understand her struggling against terrible odds to make a success of her tiny business when she lost her job with the Callahans.

Dirkson Callahan—his father.

Marc took a long pull on the beer. He couldn't believe that Dirkson was his biological father. He was a selfish man who seemed to love no one and nothing except himself, money and power.

Marc thought of his mother being pregnant, fifteen, on her own until she met his dad, no money, nothing. She didn't want to tell her parents. She hadn't wanted to rely on them because they were struggling to make a home and a life for themselves here. She'd met his real dad, the dad Marc loved and the dad who loved him. With John Medina they were a family with strong ties, and Dirkson Callahan was no part of it.

Marc took another swallow of beer, the bitter taste in his mouth not from the brew but from the mere thought of that horrible man.

He stared into the darkness. There was no reason to tell Lara, but a part of him wanted to share the news that still had him in knots. But he wouldn't. When this marriage ended, they would go their separate ways and he wouldn't see her again. And that wasn't his baby she carried.

He thought of his own child, who had been cruelly taken from him. His mom had said he wouldn't be able to walk away from Lara's baby when it was born. Was that true? For a few months he would be that baby's father. Would the child capture his heart?

And what about its mother?

He couldn't stop thinking about how he wanted Lara in his bed. How much would that complicate his life? How much would it make him want her as part of his life longer than this one year they had planned? He couldn't imagine falling in love, not when he wasn't truly over losing his wife. Would it make for a stronger tie to Lara when her baby came? That gave him pause. He needed to back off and stick to his original plan to avoid sex with her, but nights like tonight—with nothing to do but think about her—made him want her in spite of common sense and the upheaval she could cause in his life.

He finished the beer and closed his eyes on his disturbing thoughts. It was two in the morning when he woke in the darkness and moved inside, flopped on the bed and went back to sleep.

When he woke again, it was daylight. Frowning, he looked at the clock and jumped out of bed. He had overslept. Something he never did. He rushed to shower and soon was in jeans and a flannel shirt and ready for the day. As he walked down the hall, tempting smells of hot coffee and bacon frying assailed him. He rushed into the kitchen.

Lara spun around. She wore a blue cotton robe that was open and thin blue cotton pajamas beneath the robe. Her hair tumbled over her shoulders and fell freely around her face. She looked as if she had been awake only a short time.

"Good morning," he said, crossing to her, drawn as if by a magnet. Last night's warning to be cautious in getting involved with her vanished like smoke on the wind.

Her cheeks turned pink and she put down a spatula to pull her robe together. "Good morning. I figured you were long gone."

"I overslept," he said. He slipped his arm around her waist and pulled her close. She was soft and the thin cotton robe and pajamas were almost nonexistent. As her soft curves pressed against him, her eyes flew wide. "Marc, I'm not dressed."

"Yeah, I noticed and I like it. You look gorgeous," he said and kissed away her answer. For one startled second, she was still, and then her arms went around his neck and she kissed him in return.

He was hard instantly. He wanted her. He wanted to slip her out of the robe and pajamas and carry her back to bed. Instead, he stood there kissing her, relishing her softness, her warmth, her kiss that was setting him on fire.

"Marc." She finally moved out of his embrace. Her cheeks were pink and her mouth red from their kiss. "Breakfast is burning," she said, turning to grab the spatula and turn the strips of bacon. "Now look." She poked the scorched bacon.

"I'm looking," he said, his gaze roaming over her.

She put down the spatula and tied her robe. He laughed and walked away to pour himself some coffee. "I'm leaving, but I've been having breakfast by myself at the wrong time of the morning. I'll have to change that."

"And I'll have to dress for breakfast."

"Don't be ridiculous. We're married." He walked up to her to put his finger beneath her chin and tilt her face up. "Sooner or later we'll consummate this union."

"You don't know that."

"Oh, yes, I do," he said, looking into her wide blue eyes and seeing a blush turn her cheeks rosy. "You know it, too. And you want it, too. Gives us both something to look forward to. We miscalculated when we agreed on no sex. We didn't know about the attraction that would spring to life between us. We know it isn't a serious one and it isn't going to last. You still have your agenda and I have mine. But you do like to kiss and so do I."

"You don't know that we'll succumb to passion. We might and we might not," she said in a haughty tone that made him grin.

"We definitely will and you know it or you wouldn't be blushing. Want me to prove it to you right now?" he asked, walking toward her.

"No, I don't," she answered quickly, moving out of his reach.

"I think I just did," he said, laughing. "I'll see you tonight, darlin'."

Smiling, he left, but his thoughts stayed on the moment when he held her in his arms. The flimsy cotton robe and pajamas might as well have been nonexistent. She had been warm and soft. That image would be with him for the day. He couldn't resist pursuing her and she liked it when he did.

He realized he was already looking forward to being with her tonight. That was something new in his life, which, little by little, she seemed to be changing for the better. He hadn't expected to even be aware of her once they were on the ranch and each doing their own thing. Had he ever been wrong. He couldn't shake her out of his thoughts now, and that startled him. She was turning his life upside down in her own quiet way.

It occurred to him that he might miss her later, when she was gone. He shook his head as if to chase away that thought. She was a tiny, brief part of his life. He wouldn't miss her. He would go back to life the way it had been before he had brought her to the ranch. After all, that was the deal they'd made. And Marc Medina was a master of the deal.

Lara had showered and dressed in jeans and a blue knit shirt. Her hair was in one long, thick braid. She was sitting and studying when she heard a pickup, and in minutes a door slammed.

"Hi, sweetie. Your lover's home."

She had to laugh at his corny greeting. "I'm in here, in the great room."

He came through the door seeming to bring sizzling energy just by walking into the room. He had dust on his face. He had already shed his hat and jacket and wore mud-spattered jeans, muddy boots and a long-sleeved blue shirt that had some smudges of dirt and a tear.

"You look like you fell out of the pickup."

He crossed the room to her and pulled her up. "Well, you look beautiful and absolutely irresistible," he said, wrapping her in his arms and kissing away her protest until she responded in kind.

He finally released her slightly to look at her. He smelled like hay and his tousled hair fell on his forehead. He had a dark shadow of stubble on his jaw.

"Well, now I'm dusty, too," she said. "I can't get used to this marriage thing. We're sort of half-married. You kiss like it's the real thing, but then we turn around and it definitely isn't the real thing."

"It is the real thing. We had a real ceremony and we are very legally wed."

"For a little while and there's not one shred of love in this deal. And it's better that way, so back off, cowboy, before you get us both in deep trouble."

"You are really killing the fun," he said.

"Maybe so, but you'll thank me when you get to thinking about it."

She sat back down. "What about your grandfather? Did they bring him to the ranch today?"

"Change of plans. He's coming tomorrow morning, instead. At ten o'clock. That's why you didn't hear from me or see me today. I was getting their place ready."

"I'll go with you in the morning if you'd like. I can say hello to your grandmother."

"That's another thing I like about you," he said, suddenly sounding as if he meant what he said. "You're considerate."

"I understand the importance of family and losing family. I went through it with my mother, don't forget. You try to be as kind and loving as you can while you have them."

He hugged her. "There are a lot of facets to you."

"That's a new one," she said, laughing and wiggling away from him. "You did manage to kill all the cleanliness from my shower." She brushed dirt off her blouse.

"It just makes you a little earthy and sexy."

"Somehow I find cleanliness sexy."

"I'll remember that." He waggled his eyebrows at her, then tossed an envelope on the table near her. "The wedding pictures were in the mail today," he said.

She dropped everything and rushed over to pick up the envelope.

"I love pictures. I want to see. Want to come look with me?"

"Oh, sure," he said, too quickly and eagerly.

She regarded him shrewdly. "Why do I suspect your motives for looking at pictures with me?"

He grinned and she knew she was right. She shook her head as she sat on the sofa and he sat close beside her, putting his arm around her shoulders. "I can't wait to see them," he said.

"Maybe we should do this after you shower."

"I'm already here against you and seated on the sofa. I can't do more damage here, so let's look."

"I can't argue with that logic," she said and pulled out a few glossy pictures.

"You watch your hands," she said, smiling at him, and he smiled in return. Her heart beat faster because she was certain he would kiss her again soon. She shouldn't want him to, and she shouldn't let him. If she could just keep her wits about her when she was near him.

She turned back to look at the pictures. She emptied the envelope of a thick stack of prints and began to go through them. She paused to study one.

"Marc, you and Gabe look exactly alike here. Your eyes are dark brown and his are blue, but the two of you could be brothers instead of friends."

"People have told us that before," he said casually.

"Surely you can see the resemblance."

"I suppose."

"I'm sure you've met his father."

"Oh, yeah. Dirkson paid no attention to his sons. They might as well not have existed as far as he was concerned, from what Gabe always told me."

"Well, Gabe looks nothing like Dirkson Callahan. I don't think you'd know Gabe is related to him if he didn't have that Callahan name."

"That would probably suit Gabe just fine. None of the Callahan boys like him. That would be a hell of a note—none of your sons liking you, but it's his own fault. They wanted to be a family and he disappointed them and hurt them time and again."

"That's sad. He can't make it up now."

"No, those years are gone. I'll bet each one of the brothers is a fantastic dad to make up for the way Dirkson was. They never want to be like him."

She shuffled through the prints then held one up. "Ah, here's a fun picture. This one I want," she said, holding out a picture of her dancing with Marc at the reception.

"You can have all of them."

"You're going to forget me and this marriage when I'm gone," she said, laughing. "Thank you. I'll be happy to keep these pictures."

Startling her, he picked her up and placed her on his lap. "I'm not going to forget you." His arm wrapped around her waist as he pulled her close and kissed her.

She wrapped her arms around him and clung to him as she kissed him in return.

"I'm not going to forget you or this marriage. I think you're seeing to that hour by hour. That night when we went dancing, I had the best time I've had since Kathy passed away. That's unique, Lara. I'm not going to forget that."

He gazed at her solemnly as he talked and she realized he wasn't teasing. Her heart beat faster. That was awesome and made her feel better, but it scared her, too.

"I don't want to make this marriage permanent, Marc, because you never would. Don't mess up my future plans."

"We won't. We just had a good time together, and that's great because it means you're getting me out of that terrible grief I've been sunk into since I lost her. Thanks for that."

"I'm glad, Marc. There's a time to move on from being steeped in grief." As she gazed at him, she had the feeling that there had been a subtle shift in their relationship—that she had more influence on him now than she had had previously. She wasn't happy with the discovery. She didn't want to get too close to him or become too important to him. He wouldn't change when they ended this marriage and he definitely would end it. She needed to always remember that. This was a temporary situation.

She got out of his lap and warmed up the casserole she'd taken out of the freezer that morning. They ate together, and after dinner she stayed in the great room instead of fleeing to her suite. She sat with her laptop, doing her studies, while Marc sat at the desk going over the ranch books and bringing them up to date.

She finally stood as the grandfather clock chimed out in the hallway. "It's ten o'clock and I'm turning in."

Instantly Marc stood. "I will, too."

"I meant alone in my own room," she said, smiling at him.

He smiled back at her. "I tried." He shrugged. "I'll still head to my room. Now, if you ever get lonesome or change your mind—"

"I know. I'm welcome in your bed."

"Any time you want to be there. I just don't want you to forget me."

She had to laugh. "I'll try not to," she remarked. "So, what time will we go see your grandfather tomorrow?" she asked, carrying the envelope with the wedding pictures.

"Probably about eleven. If you change your mind, you don't have to go. That's not part of your duties."

"I want to. He's old and frail and he wanted this marriage badly, so I think it would make him happy to think that I'm part of the family."

"That's very nice."

"Really, it's the least I can do," she said as they

walked down the hall. At the door to her room, she turned to him. "Good night, Marc. I'll see you at breakfast in the morning."

"I hope you do. Wear the same pajamas and robe. I like them."

She shook her head at him. He really was incorrigible.

He stepped close to embrace her, ending her protest when his mouth covered hers. He pushed her back against the wall and she clung to him, returning his kiss. She couldn't say she was sorry to be trapped there. In fact, when he released her, she felt disappointed. Her breathing was as ragged as his.

"Some night you'll invite me in."

"We talked about that. I don't plan on it."

"Some night you'll invite me in," he repeated, running his forefinger down her cheek and making her heart beat faster.

She shook her head and stepped into her suite, closing the door. "Not if I have good sense, I won't," she whispered to herself, but her answer was for him. "I don't want to long for you in my bed every night and that would happen if we started sleeping together." She just prayed she wasn't already getting too attached to him.

Seven

The next morning Marc was in the great room waiting for Lara, looking out at his patio, pool and, beyond the fence, the endless vistas of the ranch. His grandfather was coming home today. Marc felt certain the old man was hanging on to see the land once more and to take his last breath on the ranch he loved.

Marc realized that life was short and that family was what was important. He thought about Lara and how she had already changed his life for the better. He hoped he had changed hers for the better, too, and enabled her to do what she wanted when they parted.

She was his wife—so far, in name only. One minute he intended to change that and the next minute he thought that if he did, he might make everything worse for both of them. He didn't want that to happen. He wanted her, but common sense warned him to stick to their original plan so no one got hurt when they parted ways. And they would part; he knew that for certain.

He heard her high heels on the hardwood floor and he stood as she swept into the room. His heart thudded. She wore a cheerful, bright-red dress with a straight skirt that ended just above her knees. She had on red high-heeled pumps and her hair was scooped up on either side of her head and pinned to fall freely in the back.

"You look gorgeous." He crossed the room to her, drawn without conscious thought. "I just can't resist, Mrs. Medina," he said, reminding her of her marital status as he wrapped his arms around her, leaned over her and kissed her.

Her eyes flew wide and then closed, and she wrapped her arms around his neck, pressed against him and kissed him in return, making his heart pound. She could be instantly responsive, and when she was, it set him on fire. He wanted her with all his being. He'd spent a restless night, tossing and turning, dreaming about her, waking and being unable to go back to sleep for a long time, arguing with himself about pursuing her.

"If we didn't have to go see my grandparents," he said, raising his head, "I would carry you off to bed."

She opened her eyes and had a dazed look that made his pulse jump another notch. "We have to go," she stated, but there wasn't any conviction in her voice. Her mouth was red from his kiss and desire filled her blue eyes.

He pulled her up to whisper in her ear. "One day I'm going to make love to you for hours and you'll want me to."

She froze in his arms and he wasn't sure what her reaction would be. Finally, she turned her head slightly and looked into his eyes. Her emotions were unreadable. She didn't pull away. Instead, she cupped his cheek in her hand and softly said, "We both know that's not the sensible thing to do. We need to get back on a safe track until we say goodbye. Goodbye is still in our lives, Marc. Now, I think we were going somewhere," she said, smoothing her dress and shaking her head to get her hair to fall back in place.

He wanted her with all his being. He was amazed by the effect she had on him. She was changing his life, hour by hour, day by day, bringing him back to life. "Marrying you was the smartest thing I ever did."

She smiled, her blue eyes getting a twinkle. "Is that so? I'm very flattered. Then I have to say, we have a good bargain."

"Yes, we do." And he needed to remember the terms of that bargain.

"Let's get going. My grandpa awaits." He put his hand on the small of her back as he ushered her out of the great room. "You know, my grandpa does like beautiful women. You'll make him happy today."

"I hope so. Your grandmother, too. Will your mom be here?"

"No, because she knows I'll handle it and she'll be at the restaurant, making sure everything is running smoothly there the way it has each day it's been open for the last thirty years." Then he paused. "At least, as far as I know, she won't be there. She surprises me sometimes."

He took his pickup, aware it was one of the few times he'd been in the truck in a suit and tie.

They arrived before his grandfather, but within ten minutes an entourage came up the road with the ambulance in the lead. Marc and Lara went out to meet the car carrying his grandmother, and Marc took her arm to help her into the guest house. Lara walked along with them, with a nurse on the other side of his grandmother.

Medics brought his grandfather in and took him to the room that Marc had made sure was ready.

Finally, Marc and Lara went to see him. Marc brushed a kiss on his grandfather's forehead and came back to stand by Lara, who greeted his grandfather.

His grandfather smiled. "You look beautiful, Lara," he said in a raspy voice.

"Thank you," she said, smiling at him. "We're glad you're home."

He nodded and folded his hands.

Marc told him about the ranch, and while he talked, he stood beside her with his arm around her waist. She was sure they looked like happily married newlyweds.

They didn't stay a long time, once they'd finished talking to his grandfather and made sure his grandmother was settled in and needed nothing. Then they said their goodbyes.

"He's happy and it was nice of you to come. He told me I married a beautiful woman," Marc said as they got into the pickup. He smiled at Lara. "He's right."

"Thank you. But I'm not sure he can see very well."

"He can see well enough. Your red dress is perfect. That would cheer up a skeleton."

"I hope I don't have to do that," she said, laughing at him.

"Hey, the guys are going out again tonight. Want to join them?"

"Sure. That was a fun evening last time."

"I hoped you'd say that. Seven tonight, then?"

"Seven it is."

When they got back to Marc's house he went inside to change to go to work.

He didn't see Lara again before he left, but tonight they would go dancing and he would be with her all evening. He had plans for afterward, too. He had already gotten a hotel room so they would not have to worry about driving back to the ranch.

Lara had more fun than she'd had the first time. This time, some of the guys politely asked her to dance. She suspected they did so to be nice to the boss's new wife, but she accepted their offers nonetheless. The evening was fun, but it was Marc who took her breath away. Tonight, his navy Western shirt was open at the throat. He had a hand-tooled leather belt with a big silver belt buckle that she suspected he'd won in a rodeo. He was charming and exciting, and when they drove to the hotel, her heart raced because she knew they would kiss.

She was supposed to be guarding her heart, so what was she doing going dancing with him and kissing him?

She had the perfect answer to that nagging voice inside her head. She wasn't in love with him and she hadn't gone to bed with him. As long as she could honestly say she wasn't in love, she would be okay. There'd be no heartbreak in her future.

When they walked up to her room, he took her key and opened her door. She entered and turned to say something to him but forgot her words when she looked up at him. His brown eyes held so much desire, she felt weak in the knees.

"You're gorgeous, Lara. I want you," he whispered as he wrapped his arms around her and pulled her against him for a heated kiss.

Kissing him in return, their tongues stroking, stirring sensations that made her moan with pleasure, she held him tightly. His waist was narrow and she could feel his hard arousal pressing against her through his thick jeans. She wanted him, too. She wanted his kisses, his hands on her, his mouth on her.

His arms tightened around her as he kissed her. In minutes he had her red blouse unbuttoned and pushed open. He unfastened her bra and cupped her breasts in his warm hands. As his thumbs circled each taut point, he stepped back to look at her.

"You're beautiful," he whispered. "I want to make love to you all night."

"Marc, you know where that will lead."

"We're married. I'm your husband. You're already pregnant. You want my hands and mouth on you just as badly as I want to kiss and make love to you. You're gorgeous, Lara, and I've wanted you all evening," he said, repeating the arguments he had given her before. He drew her to him to kiss away any protest she had.

He was right about everything. She ached for his hands and mouth on her. Would once be so terrible?

Could she go to bed with him and still say no the next time? One time didn't have to mean she would fall in love with him. Far from it.

His kiss was making it difficult to think about the consequences and the reasons she didn't want to make love. They seemed not as threatening when she was in his arms and his kisses were driving all thoughts into oblivion. She could do this and go back to life like it was. One night with him wouldn't change her life. She could say no later after this one time.

One by one, her protests crumbled.

His black hair fell in ringlets on his forehead and he had the dark shadow of stubble on his jaw. He was handsome and exciting, a man who always knew what he wanted and went after it. And he usually got it.

She was his wife and she wanted his loving, his kisses and caresses. He was fabulous in every way, exciting, handsome, sexy, fun and capable. Tonight she wanted to make love with him, to be a real wife to him. For one night. Tomorrow she would go back to a sensible restraint. One night would not change everything, she repeated to herself.

He kissed her again, passionately, his tongue stroking hers, touching the corners of her mouth, making her shake with need. His hands roamed over her, unfastening her belt and pulling it free. She barely noticed, but soon she leaned away to undo his big buckle and then unfasten his jeans and push them away. He stepped back to yank off his boots and shed his clothes, watching her as she did the same, and in minutes he'd peeled away the last of her clothes.

"You're beautiful," he said hoarsely, picking her up and carrying her into the bedroom where he yanked the covers off the bed and set her on her feet. After one long glance at her nakedness that had her skin burning, he pulled her into his embrace and kissed her again.

Her heart pounded with excitement and desire. His masculine body was perfection. She ran her hands across his broad, muscled shoulders, his hard, bulging biceps. His stomach was flat, a washboard of muscle. His manhood was thick and hard and ready to love her.

He showered kisses on first one breast and then the other, slowly circling each nipple with his warm, wet tongue, making her gasp with pleasure as her fingers tangled in his hair.

"I want to kiss you from your head to your toes," he whispered. His breath was hot on her flesh as his tongue traced circles on each breast and then moved lower over her belly and down farther. His hands played over her thighs and stroked slowly between them.

She reached between them to caress his thick rod, running her fingers over him, and then she stepped back, knelt and let her tongue stroke him. Boldly, she took him in her mouth to excite him as he had her.

He groaned, his hands tangling in her hair again as he gasped. But she did not stop.

Suddenly he reached beneath her arms to lift her up so that they faced each other. The desire that burned in his expression was so potent it made her tremble.

"You can't imagine how much I want you. You're beautiful. Every inch of you," he whispered. He picked her up and laid her on the bed, then knelt to kiss her ankle, working his way slowly up her legs. His lips blazed the trail with hot, wet kisses and his hands followed the path as they caressed every inch he'd kissed.

She moaned with need. As he moved higher, caressing her inner thighs, running his tongue over her smooth skin, she spread her legs and his fingers explored and rubbed between her thighs.

She gasped, moving her hips as he stroked her, as tension built and she sought release. She cried out, arching beneath his hands and then his mouth and tongue were on her, hot and wet and driving her wild. When she couldn't take any more of the delicious onslaught, she sat up and clutched his shoulders.

He looked up into her eyes and longing tore at her. She pulled him up, his body flush with hers, and kissed him. She locked her arms around him, holding him tightly while she poured herself into her kiss.

Each stroke, each kiss made her want him more. She couldn't touch him enough, feverishly running her hands over his marvelous male body that was all hard muscle. "You're wasting yourself in that office. This body was meant for ranch work," she whispered, trailing kisses over his flat stomach as she caressed him.

He pulled her up again to gaze at her in another long, hot, probing look and then he kissed her, a kiss she knew she would remember forever. It was a kiss that made her feel he wanted her and he cared about her. And she kissed him back, just as passionately.

He laid her back on the bed and then moved above her to continue showering kisses from her head to her toes, as he pushed her down gently whenever she attempted to kiss him or to sit up.

He turned her over and his hands drifted over her back, down over her bottom, tickling and stroking her, moving between her legs again and then pulling her up on her knees to move over her, his hands on her breasts as he trailed his tongue on her nape.

With a cry she rolled over and pulled him down on top of her.

"Love me, Marc. I want you inside me. I want us together for this night. Tonight we're husband and wife."

"I know it, Lara. Don't rush. Let's take our time. I want to start over. I want you to want me so badly, you can't possibly wait."

"I already do."

"Not like I want you to. Shh, just wait," he whispered, showering kisses on her again, taking first one breast and then the other into his mouth, kissing her all over again.

He kissed her from head to toe and then she returned the favor. His hands were still everywhere on her, tickling, stroking, teasing and loving her.

Finally she grasped his shoulders. "Now. I want you now," she said, looking intently at him.

He moved between her legs as she watched him. Her heart raced, she wanted him so badly. She ran her hands over his muscled thighs, feeling the short, crisp, curly hairs against her palms.

He lowered his weight, entering her gradually. With a muffled cry as he kissed her, she wrapped her long legs around him and ran her hands over his back and hard buttocks.

He filled her, thick and hot, making her arch beneath him and cry out for him. "Love me." She gasped as she arched her hips against him, higher and higher, wanting more.

He held back, drawing out their loving while she writhed beneath him, wanting him more by the second. Each thrust was torment and ecstasy.

Her eyes were closed tightly as she clung to him, holding him with one arm while her other hand ran over his hard body.

He began to move his hips, thrusting and withdrawing, repeating it as she moved with him until, finally, he lost control and began to pump hard and fast.

With a cry she moved with him, arching her hips higher, tightening her legs around him as she moved wildly and her head thrashed back and forth.

"Marc, I want you," she cried.

They built to a crisis and finally spilled over a brink that was shattering. Lights exploded behind her closed eyes and she rocked hard and fast with him while rapture enveloped her.

Groaning, Marc held her tightly, thrusting hard and reaching his climax.

They slowed gradually, gasping for breath until they were finally still. Marc rolled to his side, keeping her with him as he caught locks of her hair and pushed them away from her face. He placed his hand at her throat and she knew he could feel her racing pulse.

"See what you do to me?" she whispered.

"My pulse is just as fast," he said. "We do that to each other." He showered light kisses on her ear, her throat, her cheek. "You're marvelous, Lara. This has been a fabulous night. I want you to stay right here in my bed, in my arms, all night long," he said as she wound her arms around him and held him.

"It was good, Marc," she said, kissing him lightly, her fingers wandering over his smooth back. She wanted to hold him all night.

"I want you to stay with me tonight. Don't go," he repeated.

"I'm not moving. I'm not going anywhere out of your arms," she whispered. Ecstasy, euphoria, happiness filled her, and for a moment in time, she felt wanted and loved. She held him in her arms and wished she never had to let go. She knew that was impossible, but for a few more minutes, this was paradise.

She had no idea how late it was when she woke in his arms. Needing a bathroom break, she slipped out from beside his sleeping body.

When she returned to the bed, he stirred. "Don't go."

She didn't bother correcting him. Instead, she burrowed against him. "That suits me."

While he kissed her throat, she clung to him, twisting her fingers in his chest hair.

"I don't want to let you go," he whispered as he tightened his arms around her.

"But you will let me go," she said quietly, wondering how much their relationship had changed tonight and how significant making love would be in their lives.

"Shh. No tomorrows. Tonight you're in my arms, in my bed, and I want you to stay."

"And tonight, that's fine with me," she said. Their

legs were intertwined and she felt as close as she could get to him. "We've been good together, Marc."

"I think so. I think asking you to marry me was one of the best things I've ever done. You're perfect and you've made my grandparents and my mom happy. And all that family happiness—and some of my own—is going to make our breakup hurt a little. My mom isn't going to like it when we break up. I'm going to hurt her and I don't want to do that."

"I suppose that's unavoidable since you couldn't find someone you really loved and wanted forever."

"Not in one month," he remarked.

She didn't say anything about how she would feel when Marc divorced her and the marriage of convenience was over.

As he held her close, they stopped talking and lay together, holding each other and caressing each other. She knew when the moment changed and he wanted to make love again.

In seconds, his arms tightened around her and he leaned down to kiss her. She slipped her arms around his neck and kissed him in return. She didn't think it was possible, but in no time he had her wanting him as much as she had earlier in the evening. They made love again, taking even longer than the time before.

Midmorning she stirred and looked around to find him propped on his hand looking at her. He smiled at her. "That was a fantastic night."

"And long over. I think we better shower and go home. Are all those guys here who work for you?"

"I have no idea where they are. I haven't stepped out of this bed since the sun came over the horizon, but I imagine they're long gone. But not to worry. They know we're newlyweds."

"That's a little embarrassing. Your car is still here."

"We're married. What's wrong with us staying in for a while?"

She laughed. "I don't feel very married."

He caught her hand and held up her ring finger. "I'd say that's very married."

"Yes, you're right when you put it that way," she agreed when she looked at the diamonds glittering on her finger. She sat up, pulling the sheet to her chin, aware of him with the sheet over his hips, his skin looking darker than ever against the white sheets.

"I'm going to shower and dress. We should go home. I have an assignment that's due Monday that I need to work on."

"Do you really?" he asked, pulling her down against his chest. He was warm, and his intense look made her heart miss beats. "I have a better idea. You come here, and in a few minutes we'll both go shower. In the meantime, I want a morning kiss," he said, shifting and turning on his side, pulling her closer and kissing her.

The minute his mouth touched hers, she forgot

her protest. His arms tightened around her and she wrapped her arms around him, clinging to him, pressing against him, feeling the chest hairs against her bare breasts. She wanted him again, was ready to make love. She didn't want to get out of bed and have the idyll end.

Last night she had felt really married, desired by him, loved by him, a part of his life. They'd had fun all evening, and then making love locked them into intimacy, shifted their relationship to something much more important, much deeper for her. It was an illusion that she didn't want to end yet. Their marriage was real, but not based on love and it would not last. She had had her moment with him. Now she needed to step away before she made herself far more vulnerable to hurt. She had to say no to him after this. If she lived as his wife the rest of the time with him, the divorce would hurt terribly. It would break her heart.

This was a fling and it would end—right after this.

He kissed her, his tongue going deep, stroking her mouth, stirring and arousing her until she moaned softly and ran her hands over him, moving her hips against him.

He shifted, throwing aside the sheet to uncover both of them, getting on his knees and moving between her legs. She gazed into his eyes and saw desire blazing in their depths. He wanted her and he was ready to love again.

She wrapped her legs around him as he entered her slowly, making her gasp with pleasure as she arched beneath him and clung to him tightly. He withdrew, only to enter her again and again, filling her deeper each time until she went over the edge. She cried out, clutching his butt, pulling him to her as she thrashed beneath him and he began to pump faster.

She held him tightly while she climaxed, hearing his moan and knowing he reached a climax also.

Finally they were still, locked together, holding each other while she opened her eyes to look at him.

"Now I can't move."

"Good. I don't want you to move anyway. I want you here in my arms. You know I can get this room for the day."

She laughed. "Don't you dare. We need to get back to the ranch. I have things to do."

"You don't have anything nearly as important as making me happy," he said, and she laughed.

"That's a hoot. There might be a thing or two that comes before you and your well-being."

"Be careful or you'll hurt my feelings," he teased. He rose up on his arm to look down at her. "See, we can have a good time together in bed. We can have a really good time together naked in bed. Move into my suite when we get back to the ranch."

"Marc, this has been fantastic, but I can't move in with you knowing that this will end and that we don't love each other. I don't want a broken heart. I don't want a temporary relationship and you don't want a permanent marriage—which I understand. This is a business arrangement with papers. It's a contract marriage of convenience. I can't move in with you and I can't sleep with you anymore. We did and it was wonderful. But we have to stop now while I can still say goodbye."

"Think about it, Lara. You know you enjoy my company."

She shook her head. "I don't think you're listening to me."

"We're married. Why can't we live together?"

"You know there's no love in this marriage. That is an enormous difference in everything we do with each other."

"True, but we aren't going to fall in love."

"If I start sleeping in your bed with you, it'll be a possibility for me, and you'll still want a divorce."

"But you won't fall in love. You have all that cool control you exhibit all the time. You'll be in charge of your feelings and just because you're in my bed, you won't necessarily be any wilder about me than you are now."

"That I would seriously doubt."

He hugged her and smiled at her, combing long strands of her hair away from her face with his fingers. "All joking aside, you've got me beyond that terrible grief. I'm so amazed because I've lived with that since I lost Kathy and I had sort of accepted it as a way of life. What's funny—you didn't consciously try to do that. It just happened. I've come back to life. It's fun to be with you and it's relaxed. You haven't tried to make me fall in love with you. Far from it," he added and she smiled.

"We went into this marriage knowing we would not fall in love with each other and we would divorce later this year. That makes a difference in how we deal with each other. And moving in with you definitely won't work."

"I don't know that it made such a damn big difference last night."

"Maybe not. Last night was an exception," she said. "I think it would make it more painful to divorce if we're together a lot and living and sleeping together and making love. That doesn't seem the way to stay on track for a divorce. I have plans for my future and I don't want to be in upheaval and turmoil because of a heartbreak." She shook her head. "Besides, you think I'm driven and I put work first and you don't like that. You didn't like it with your mother. Frankly, I think you're just as driven. I think that would cause all kinds of trouble between us. I think—"

He stopped her rant with a finger to her lips. "Don't take life so seriously, Lara."

She pushed his finger away. "I have to. I'm having a baby, Marc, remember?" She had to think of her child in addition to her own future. "And I don't hear you denying it. I doubt if you like my determination to become a doctor."

Her secretarial work had been fine with him, but to devote herself to a demanding career that took extra hours of work, he had made it clear many times before that he didn't like that. And she didn't want an emotional entanglement with another man who didn't agree with her life choices.

"I didn't say I didn't like it."

She pressed him. "Do you want to be married to someone going to medical school? To a doctor?"

He ran a hand through his dark curls. "It's beside the point because we're not staying together forever. If you want an answer, no, I wouldn't want my wife to be a doctor. I've had that all my life with my mother tied to her work. You're blowing this out of proportion. I just asked you to move in with me."

"If I did, we would have this conversation down the road." She sat up, feeling the chill that came with leaving his arms. "Sorry, Marc, I'm not moving in with you."

She drew in a deep breath and looked down at him. "We're just not compatible. Look how we're arguing now. Right after we've made love all night. No, moving in with you will just cause more problems and interfere in our futures." Her voice echoed the dejection she felt. "Marc, there is no love in this, don't you see? You're not in love with me and I'm not in love with you. And we're getting divorced eventually. You're still planning on a divorce, aren't you?"

"Yes, I am." He paused and his gaze deepened, his eyes roving over every inch of her face, as if to memorize her. "I've got your answer—you're not moving in. So why, after all that, do I still want to kiss you?" He pulled her down to him, but she placed her hands against his chest.

"Are you paying attention at all? We should be putting distance between us instead of staying in bed and kissing."

"Why don't you forget that divorce for ten minutes?"

He looked at her mouth and against every shred of good judgment she felt her insides tighten. He brushed her lips with his, lightly, yet her heart surged. Every part of her knew this was wrong, but she couldn't stop it, the desire she felt when his mouth settled on hers. His tongue stroked hers and, as if of their own volition, her arms wrapped around him and she kissed him back. With one kiss she forgot their conversation and all her arguments.

It was midafternoon when they finally packed and returned to the ranch. As they entered the house, tempting smells of a pot roast filled the air.

"Ah, come meet my cook," he said, putting their

things by the door. He took her arm as they walked to the kitchen.

"Penelope, I'm home and I want you to meet my new wife."

A short woman with curly red hair turned and smiled. She wore a blue cotton apron that covered her from her neck to her ankles. Her blue eyes filled with curiosity.

"Penelope, this is Lara Medina. Lara, meet Penelope Wendell."

Lara offered her hand. "I'm glad to meet you. It smells wonderful in this kitchen."

Penelope's smile widened as they shook hands. "Pot roast for supper tonight. It will be ready about six."

"That's great," Marc said. "We'll eat about seven, so just leave it and we can get it on the table." He turned to Lara. "Penelope has been with us for fifteen years. She worked for my grandparents first. She's been with me the past four years. She works in Dallas or here on the ranch."

"I'm anxious to taste that pot roast," Lara said. They talked briefly and then left to take their things upstairs.

As they walked down the hall, she asked him, "Why do you want to return to the corporate world? Why don't you stay on the ranch? You seem way happier and more relaxed since you've been here. The problems you have here don't seem to get you down as much as the ones at the Dallas office."

"I like making money in the corporate world. I like the challenges. Maybe I am happier here. I hadn't really thought about it. I didn't have you in my bed before, so maybe that's making me happy."

She shook her head at him. "Marc—"

But he quickly changed the subject. "This afternoon I'm going to see my grandparents."

"I'll go if you think they'd like to see me."

"I think they would. As far as they're concerned, you're part of the family now. A pretty lady is sure to cheer up my grandfather. You know, in her day my grandmother was a beauty. At least, she looked quite pretty in her pictures."

Lara smiled at him. "Let me get cleaned up. I don't want to go like this."

"Want to shower together?"

She laughed as she shook her head. "I don't think we would ever get there if we shower together first."

"Meet you here in…what? An hour? Half an hour?"

"Half an hour," she said and walked with him to their rooms, leaving him to go into her suite and close the door.

When they returned from their visit, she knew he would bring up moving in with him again before the evening was over. Had her decision changed since this morning in Downly? She'd better make up her mind once and for all and stick with it. Vacillating wasn't helping anyone. "No" was the safe and smart thing to tell him. Did she want to risk her heart for sex with Marc or did she want to play it safe as she had promised herself she would do?

No pressure. Only her future was at stake.

Eight

Marc laughed as he went to his room. He was having fun with Lara, but he was serious when he urged her to move in with him. He wanted her in his bed, in his arms at night. He wanted to hold her and make love and have her with him. He had surprised himself when he blurted out the invitation to move in with him.

He hadn't given it thought ahead of time—something so unlike himself that he had been shocked. She was changing him, changing his life. He had a feeling she wasn't trying to do so, it was just happening with her around.

He also had a feeling that he was a small part of

her life, not the focus, which was something that usually didn't happen to him with his women friends. Lara had plans for her life, goals. She was more interested in adding *Doctor* to her name than *Mrs.* And he'd best remember that, he reminded himself. Despite his physical attraction to her, she was not the woman for him with her drive to tie her life to her work.

But the sex…

The sex he'd had with Lara had been the best he'd ever experienced. Another shocker. She was intensely responsive and she had an enthusiasm for lovemaking that made everything more exciting and sexy.

He realized he better change his train of thought because he had to get ready to go see his grandparents, and thinking about sex with Lara wasn't the way to do it.

In twenty minutes, dressed in gray slacks and a charcoal sport coat, he went down to the great room to wait for Lara. He stood when he heard her heels and she swept into the room, taking his breath away.

"Oh, you do know how to dress for my grandparents," he said, looking at her bright blue dress. The neckline was high, which would please his grandmother. The hemline was high, too, which would please his grandpa. She wore the necklace he had given her, and high-heeled blue pumps, and her hair fell freely around her face.

"You look stunning," he said quietly.

"Thank you. You look very nice yourself."

He pulled on the cuffs of his white dress shirt, the gold cufflinks catching glints of sunlight. Then he took her arm and led her down the hall. "They're looking forward to seeing us. I talked to Grandma. She repeated how glad they are to be home. She thanked me for getting them home."

"I'm glad, Marc. Does it worry you that our marriage won't be permanent like he wants?"

"No, because he shouldn't tell me to get a wife and get married in one month. He wasn't himself and he wasn't thinking it through. I know he always thinks he knows what's best for me, but I'm a grown man and I can make my own choices. Anyway, you and I have worked things out, and we'll be happy and he's happy. And, once again, this is nice of you to come with me to see them."

"Oh, sure. That's a small thing."

"Maybe, but I just want you to know I appreciate it."

He held the door as she stepped into his pickup, and he couldn't help but glance down at her endless legs.

When they arrived at his grandparents' place, they greeted his grandmother first. When Marc held her shoulders lightly and kissed her cheek, she felt so frail, it made his heart lurch.

"Would Grandpa like to see both of us or just me?"

"Both of you, of course," his grandmother answered. "Come with me and we'll say hello. He'll want to see your beautiful bride," she said, smiling at Lara who smiled in return.

"Thank you, Mrs. Ruiz."

After greeting the nurse on duty, they stepped into a room with the sound of a monitor beeping, keeping track of Marc's grandfather's vital signs.

"Hi, Grandpa," Marc said, taking Lara's arm and moving to the bed.

"Marc and his bride are here to see you, Papa," Grandma said, and he waved his hand.

"Get a chair."

"I have a chair. Lara, would you like to sit here?" Marc asked.

She said hello to his grandfather and sat in the chair near the bed. Marc stood behind her.

"How are you feeling today?" Marc asked him.

His grandfather looked at Lara. "Do you love my grandson?"

"I married him, sir," she said.

Marc wondered what his grandfather was up to. There were moments he could be quite shrewd and Marc wondered if he had guessed that Marc wasn't in love with Lara.

"I hear you have no family at all."

"Not until I married your grandson. Now Marc's family is my family. Isn't that right?"

His grandfather smiled at her. "You're part of our family and we welcome you."

"Thank you," she answered.

Marc placed his hand on her shoulder, wondering if his grandfather's questions disturbed her.

"Let me see the rings Marc gave you."

She stood and held out her hand, and his grandfather took it in his, rubbing his thumb across her fingers.

"Soft hands," he said. "Very beautiful hands. Beautiful diamonds that mean he loves you very much."

Rico released her. "I hope you and my grandson will always love each other. You took a vow to do that."

"Yes, sir, we did," she replied, sitting in her chair again and crossing her legs, a motion that caught his grandfather's glance.

"You're a beautiful woman, and you and Marc should have beautiful children. Marc was a beautiful child."

"I'll bet he was," she said, laughing. "And thank you for the compliment."

Grandpa smiled at her and Marc shook his head realizing she was not intimidated in the least by his grandfather and his questions.

"Today must be a better day," Marc said, and his grandmother nodded.

"It is a better day and he has rallied some, they tell us."

"Good. Maybe it's from being home."

They talked for another fifteen minutes and then Marc stood and said goodbye. In a short time they were back in the pickup for the drive home.

"I don't know what some of Grandpa's questions were about, especially that remark that we vowed to love each other."

"He may have guessed what you're doing—a marriage of convenience."

"I'm glad he didn't intimidate you. I think he was trying to."

She smiled. "I thought he was adorable. And I feel like part of your family, Marc, even though common sense tells me that I'm certainly not. They've been so welcoming and I guess I just want a family."

Marc sensed her mood change and lightened the tone. "Grandpa—adorable?"

Lara laughed and he loved the sight of her smile. Loved that he made her smile. "I'm glad you went with me," Marc said, and meant it.

"I'm glad I did, too."

He parked at the back of the house under the carport and they entered the great room. The minute he closed the door behind her, he reached out, caught her hand and pulled her into his arms.

"I can't wait one minute longer."

She placed her fingers on his lips, stopping his kiss. "Marc, you'll only make parting much more difficult."

"Stop worrying about tomorrow. You'll go to school and get the career you want. Hell and high water won't stop you."

"I've told you, Marc, it's a tribute to my mom. I want to help people like her—through medicine, through research, whatever works out. It's for my mother and makes me feel part of her is with me."

He nodded. "That's admirable. You're really dedicated to it."

"Yes, I am," she admitted. She smiled at him. "I don't think you get it, but you work just as hard."

"It doesn't seem the same to me."

"That's because you're not really looking at yourself."

"I'll guarantee you, you're more interesting." He pulled her closer, till she was flush against him. "In the meantime, you look gorgeous and it's been way too long since I held you and kissed you." His mouth took hers and he kissed away any answer she might have had.

The kiss was worth waiting for.

But as he was about to make his next move, Lara stepped back.

"I think we need to catch our breath. I'll put dinner on. I can't wait to try that pot roast."

"I'll get a beer and get you a lemonade, and then we can sit and talk while it heats up. How's that sound?"

"Like another good deal," she said. "I'll see you

in a few minutes. I'm going to go change first." She left him to enter her suite and close the door. As she changed, she thought about moving in with him as he wanted her to do. She had wanted to say yes—oh, how she had wanted to—but wisdom said no. She needed to keep enough distance from him that she didn't make this marriage seem real to herself. He'd never fall in love with her and she couldn't risk her heart by falling in love with him.

On the other hand, if she moved in with him, he might not ever want her to move out.

She laughed at herself and shook her head. How many women had slept with men because each one convinced herself that she was the woman he would want forever and ask to stay? The world was filled with women who'd had that foolish thought and she didn't want to become a statistic.

She went downstairs and they had dinner out on the patio. Afterward they talked for hours, until darkness fell. And before she knew what was happening, Marc rose from his chair and picked her up to carry her to his big bedroom.

During the night she stirred and turned to look at him, holding her close against his side as he slept. Was she already falling in love with him?

If she was, there wasn't any way to stop it. He wanted her in his bed at night and she wanted to be there. Her gaze ran over him and her pulse quickened. How long would he have that effect on her? She suspected it would be for as long as she knew him.

She realized now that no matter what she did, the divorce was going to hurt. On the other hand, she would move on with her life and now her financial worries were gone, thanks to Marc.

She shifted slowly, trying to avoid disturbing him, and propped her head on her hand to look at him. He excited her. He was incredibly handsome and sexy, more so now than he had been before their marriage. Or was she just in love and dazzled by him?

She wanted to run her hand over Marc's chest, but he was a light sleeper and she was afraid her touch would wake him.

"Like what you see?" he drawled, startling her.

She looked at him. His eyes were still closed.

"How did you know I was looking at you? Your eyes are closed."

"Magic. Besides, I know you find me fascinating," he said and grinned. He pulled her down onto his chest and kissed her, ending their conversation.

Later, she lay in his arms, pressed against him.

"Lara, I feel I can trust you and I want to share something with you that's worrying me. You have a sensible view of the world and I want your take on something. But what I tell you has to end with you."

"Sure. It sounds serious."

"It is serious. Because you're pregnant and it's not my baby, when I told my mom, she got very upset."

Lara sat up to look down at him. "Oh, Marc. She doesn't want me married to you."

"Don't be ridiculous. Mom loves you and loves that I'm married to you. You're already really a part of my family and I want your opinion on a family thing that I'm worried about. Just listen."

They both sat up and she turned to face him. Her eyes had adjusted to the dim light of the one small table lamp that was on in the room. His eyes, she saw, were dark and somber as he related what his mother told him.

"Oh, Marc. Dirkson Callahan is your blood father," she said. "I am so sorry, but thank heavens he wasn't part of your life. Have you told Gabe?"

"No. Besides Mom and Dirkson, you and I are the only other people to know. Gabe is already my best friend so I don't think I should tell him. This is what worries me, because I want to do what's best for Gabe. What do you think?"

She looked away, thinking it over. She glanced back to see him watching her. "Thank you for confiding in me," she said. "That makes me feel very close to you. Maybe even important to you."

"You are important to me and you're trustworthy and you're levelheaded. I value your opinion."

She lapsed into silence while she thought about what he had told her. "You said Blake is a half brother."

"Yes, he is. He was good friends with Cade. Dirkson never acknowledged Blake until after he was married and even then, Blake called Dirkson. Cade drew Blake into the family circle of brothers. Cade isn't quite as close as I am with Gabe. In a way, I feel like leaving them alone. We're all close anyway."

She sat thinking about it. "Well, you told me because you want my opinion, so I'm going to give it to you. I have no family, so family seems the most important thing there is for anyone. You and Gabe are blood brothers. I think you should tell him and let him decide if he wants to keep it to himself."

Marc clamped his lips together. "Well, I wanted your opinion. I'll still think about it, but you've got a strong point for telling him. I'll tell you, as far as I'm concerned, my real dad is John Medina. He was a wonderful dad and I loved him, and I hate claiming Dirkson, even to tell Gabe."

"I understand. You'll make the best choice, I'm sure."

"Enough about that. I think now we should talk about what makes me happy in bed."

She laughed and kissed his throat. "I'm beginning to find out. Actually, you're rather easy to please."

"Am I ever," he said, pulling her in for a kiss.

For the next two weeks she slept in his room at night. Marc wondered if he would ever tire of her.

He couldn't imagine that happening. One night, as he held her in his arms after making love, he toyed with her hair. "I've never brought a woman to the ranch until you. I mean, someone I was going out with. I'm not talking about Mom."

Lara turned on her side to look at him. "Really? I'm flattered, I guess. Unless you didn't bring them because you seldom came yourself."

"Oh, no. I've been here plenty. I haven't taken anyone home with me in Dallas, either. I go with them so I can leave."

"That makes sense and sounds like you."

"Well, I thought you might find that fact flattering, that I brought you home with me."

"Not exactly, because you married me. You had to take me with you. We really have a business deal between us."

He laughed. "I guess you can look at it that way."

"You had no choice." She ran her fingers along his jaw and when the moonlight caught the glitter of diamonds on her hand, she grew pensive. Finally she said, "How long have your grandparents been married?"

"A thousand years," he answered. "Actually, how's sixty-three?"

"Impossible. I can't remotely imagine."

He nodded. "A long time." He pulled long locks of her hair through his fingers and let them fall. He loved the feel of her silky strands and loved when she wore it down for him. "I've been thinking about us. Lara, let's just separate for a while instead of divorcing, and see how that works and if we want to go ahead with the divorce."

She shook her head. "No. When it's over, it's over and we'll each go on with our lives."

"I have a feeling that I'm not very important to you," he said.

"You're incredibly important, but I know you're not going to want to stay together."

"I want to stay together now. I don't want to get out of this bed today. Maybe this week," he said, rolling over on top of her and letting his kiss keep her right where he wanted her.

That morning, when she stirred Marc had already gone. Lara slipped out of bed and went to her suite to shower and dress. She moved routinely, her thoughts on her husband. She was falling in love with him and every night she spent in his bed made that love just a bit stronger.

She had to end it before she was so in love with him it would hurt forever. He was everything wonderful—handsome, intelligent, sexy, caring, fun, strong and filled with energy and enthusiasm for life. She had intended to guard her heart, and then she had turned around and fallen into his arms and into his bed, and now she was in love with him.

He didn't want a lasting marriage and she had to

follow her plans, ones that he really didn't like. She had to get off the ranch, get her life together. Marc wouldn't change. And neither would she.

She knew he didn't approve of the time she put in to become a doctor. But she'd never give up her goal because it was so tied to her love for her mother. She couldn't shake the feeling that she'd failed her mother when she hadn't been able to stop the disease that killed her. Mark didn't get how important her career was to her, yet his career was essential to him. He thought she was a workaholic like his mother, but ironically he was one himself, but he didn't recognize that.

She needed to go back to Dallas for a while and get some space between them before she was hopelessly in love with him. And she prayed that hadn't already happened.

A few days later Lara was pouring over a book when the phone rang. It was Marc's landline and only his mother and grandparents used it. She answered and thought someone had the wrong number because the noise was garbled. She started to hang up and then realized someone was crying. There were scrambling noises, words she couldn't catch, but then someone spoke clearly. "Is Marc Medina there?"

"No. Have you tried his cell phone?"

"Yes, and he didn't answer. This is the nurse and we need to get in touch with him."

"I'll text him right now and get him to call you," Lara said, replacing the phone. She grabbed her cell phone to send Marc a text. She couldn't shake the chill that overcame her, afraid that something had happened to his grandfather.

In minutes Marc called her. "I'm on my way home. My grandpa died this morning. I'll come home and get you, and we'll go over there to see Grandma. Mom's on her way, too. You don't have to go, Lara, if you don't—"

She interrupted him. "Marc, I'm getting ready now. I'll be ready when you get here. I'm so sorry. Is there anything I can do for you?"

"No. See you soon."

Then he was off the phone and she quickly went to change, pulling on a tailored black dress and putting her hair up in a bun at the back of her head the way she used to wear it to the office.

She heard his pickup and heard him running to the door. He swept inside and she ran to him. "I'm sorry, Marc."

"Thanks. I want to get over there as soon as I can and I hope I can get there before Mom does. Someone is driving her out here. I'll be ready in ten minutes."

"Can I do anything?"

He just shook his head as he left the room.

They spent the next couple of days with relatives

and getting ready for the service. It was a whirlwind of activity leading up to what was a solemn funeral.

When they walked into Marc's darkened house after the burial, he switched on the lights. She crossed the great room to him and slid her arms around his waist. "There's nothing else I can tell you, Marc, except that I'm sorry for your loss. I know how much you loved him."

He placed his head against hers and stood in her embrace. "Thank you," he whispered, and from the sound of his voice she realized he was finally giving in to his grief.

After a few minutes he raised his head while he still held her. "Thanks for going with me and for all your help through this."

"Of course. I'm glad I got to know him."

Marc released her and wiped his eyes. He walked over to the window and looked out at the lighted pool. "I think he hung on to get home to the ranch and to see me married. You're probably right. He probably guessed we just had a marriage of convenience. He seemed happy enough, though. You impressed him. He liked you." As he talked, Marc shed his coat and tie, and partially unbuttoned his shirt while he kicked off his shoes.

"We didn't have much time with each other, but I hope he liked me. I liked him."

"I promise he liked you. I think he wanted you to stay in the family."

"That's nice, Marc. Well, now you'll have your ranch and your inheritance. And your mom will, too. Will she retire?"

"Put yourself in her place. Would you retire?"

She smiled. "Be glad she's active."

"Neither you nor my mom know how to let go and enjoy life."

"I have to do what I have to do. I know we will divorce."

His gaze was stormy and she shivered, suddenly feeling as if the marriage was already disintegrating. "You'll have your divorce and you can go to med school, but tonight I want to say goodbye." He crossed the room to pick her up, carrying her to a bedroom while he kissed her, a demanding, possessive kiss that made her heart race. He stood her on her feet, peeling away her black dress as he kissed her and then flinging aside his shirt and belt. He stepped back to look at her.

"You take my breath away. You're so beautiful—every inch of you. I want you. I don't want you to go, but I know you're going to school no matter what and we're going to have to say goodbye. Tonight I need you. I want your kisses and I want to touch and kiss you."

Her heart thudded and desire overrode all her other feelings. It had been an emotional day and tomorrow might even be more emotional because, any time now, she knew they would part. She wanted to give Marc a night that would make him remember her. And she wanted to take memories with her when she said goodbye. She loved him and she knew he wasn't in love with her. Tonight he was hurting and angry she was going, but she couldn't stay. There had never been words of love from him. She wrapped her arms around his neck and kissed him, pouring her feelings into her kiss, wanting to drive away both his demons and hers.

He made a sound deep in his throat and his right hand tangled in her hair while he cupped her breast with his other hand, his thumb circling lightly, slowly around her nipple, making her moan with desire and pleasure.

Running her tongue over his male nipples, first one and then the other, she wanted to heighten his pleasure. He gasped and his hand was still tangled in her hair while he caressed her breast in feathery strokes that made her tremble with longing for more. As she ran her tongue over him, she slowly slid down until she took his thick rod in her hand, stroking him with her tongue, taking him in her mouth. She felt him shudder and gasp while she slipped one hand between his legs to caress him. He grew even larger with every touch.

He moaned and reached beneath her arms to pull her to her feet. She gazed into his dark eyes, which blazed with so much desire she couldn't get her breath.

"Marc," she whispered while wrapping her arms around him and kissing him. Her heart pounded so violently she wondered if he felt it as he held her pressed against him. His strength, his maleness, his caresses and kisses all drove her wild. She loved him, but she wasn't going to tell him when he didn't love her in return.

She put one leg up around him and he slipped his hand beneath her thigh to pick her up and lay her on the bed. He moved between her legs, caressing her with his fingers before using his mouth. He drew his hot, wet tongue over her, taking his time. Her hips arched beneath his touch.

"Marc, I want you," she whispered.

He stretched on the bed beside her and easily lifted her on top of him. She sat astride him as he caressed her breasts.

Closing her eyes, she gasped with pleasure. For a moment she was still, relishing his hands on her body, his caresses that heightened desire. Finally, she leaned down to kiss him while he held her hips and moved her over him, his thick manhood easing inside her slowly. Crying out with need and pleasure, she tossed her head, her hair swinging over her shoulder as she rode him and he held her.

Her eyes flew open while he toyed with her breasts and then both of them were moving, faster and faster, as he pumped inside her. Need for release, for all of him, hot and wet, consumed her. The spiral increased until she cried out as she went over the brink. Seconds later, he reached his climax, shuddering and thrusting fast and hard, driving her to another climax. Finally she fell on top of him, turning her head to look at him as she shifted her hips and moved so they were no longer one.

When she did, he wrapped his arms around her, holding her close.

"You can't know what a gift you just gave me," he whispered, leaning closer to brush a light kiss on her forehead. "You've demolished me, but you drove away the demons for a little. You're a fantastic woman, Lara," he whispered.

"I wanted to make you forget your hurt for just a little while. And I wanted to make sure you'll remember me."

"I couldn't possibly forget you. Tonight you took me to another place, and our loving held the pain at bay."

"I'm glad," she whispered.

Silence came and in the quiet her thoughts were in turmoil. She had to face the truth. She had fallen in love with him and there was no future for them except divorce. Their last kiss was her kiss goodbye.

Hours later, after Marc had gone to sleep, she lay awake in the dark, thinking about the changes that would be coming. They'd go ahead now with the divorce and she would move back to Dallas. There she'd keep taking chemistry courses that would count toward a doctorate in chemistry in case she didn't get into med school. When her baby was six months or a year, she would see about going to school, but at this point, she felt she needed to give her attention to her baby.

Tears stung her eyes because she loved Marc with her whole heart. She had never been in love to this extent before. Breaking her engagement to Leonard Crane had been relatively easy because she hadn't been that deeply in love, and when he wanted to have an abortion, she'd known he wasn't the man for her. But Marc had really captured her heart. Until she left the ranch, she was going to have a difficult time keeping her true feelings hidden from him, but she had to. Nothing good could come from him knowing how deeply in love with him she was.

She hurt all over at the thought of telling him goodbye. But there wasn't any reason for her to stay on the ranch now. He had said he wanted to be there when she had her baby, but she couldn't live months with him or into more than a year and then say goodbye. That would be far more devastating than now and this was terrible. She had to face him and tell him she was leaving.

At breakfast the next morning, she got to the kitchen early so she could catch him. Shortly after, he came in. He usually brought an energy and vitality into the room, but this morning he wore a slight frown.

She wasted no time but went straight into the speech she'd prepared in the wee hours of the morning. "I wanted to talk to you. I know you have a lot of legal things to do to settle your grandfather's estate, but this is important. We're still headed toward divorce, but there's no reason now for me to stay on the ranch. Whether we divorce now or not, I'm going back home to Dallas, Marc."

His frown deepened and he gazed at her in silence for a moment. "I suppose I should have known that's what you'd want to do. When do you want to go?"

She hurt inside, a tight knot in her throat, and she battled tears. He didn't even try to stop her or say he wanted her to stay a while longer. She might have been able to compromise if there was love and acceptance, but he'd simply asked when she wanted to go. That hurt, but it shouldn't have surprised her. He was letting her go as he'd always said he would.

"I'll get your things moved, so don't worry about that. Just pack and leave them. You can take the limo to Dallas. I'll get your car loaded and one of my guys can drive your car. That'll be easier for you."

"I'm ready," she managed to say. "I don't really have that much here at the ranch."

He crossed the room to her and placed his hands on her shoulders. "I know you have to go. I'd like to be around when your baby is born, but life may change a lot by then."

She nodded, because she couldn't speak. Tears had blocked her throat.

"I'll miss you, Lara."

She looked up into his stormy dark-brown eyes and wondered what he was really feeling. Would he just miss her in bed? She had to get away from him before she started crying and couldn't stop.

"I'll miss you, too," she choked out. She brushed past him and hurried to her suite, leaving him standing there. He was letting her go, just as he had told her he would from the very first.

Even in her suite she fought back her tears. She wouldn't cry until she could get away from the ranch.

His words hurt because he didn't sound as if breaking up their marriage disturbed him. And why would it? She was the one who had lost her heart—just what she didn't want to do.

It was noon before the limo and her car were packed and ready. She stood looking at herself in the mirror in her suite. She wore her red dress and let her hair fall around her face. She wondered when she would see him again—in divorce court?

Leaving him hurt her more than she had dreamed possible, but she straightened her shoulders, drew in a breath and walked out of her room.

Marc sat on the back porch by the portico, waiting for her. When she stepped out, he came to his feet. The limo was ready and Randall, one of his ranch hands, waited by the passenger door with his back to them.

She turned to Marc. "I'll see you in Dallas."

"Yeah, I'll call you. We're not saying goodbye yet. I'll see you in the city and I'll take you to dinner soon." He walked closer. "We don't have to rush this divorce, Lara. I still want to be there when you have your baby. Mom will want to be there, too. She'll help you with your baby if you'll let her."

"You know that's wonderful for me. I'd like for both of you to be with me," she said, surprised that was still what he wanted to do.

"I want to stay in your life when you have your baby."

"Sure, Marc," she said, doubting if he would continue to feel that way next spring.

"We'll see each other and stay in touch," he said.

She nodded. She couldn't talk because she would start crying. "Bye, Marc," she said. She couldn't kiss him either. She merely turned and rushed for the limo, hurrying around to climb inside while Randall closed the door behind her. She didn't look back as they drove away. She turned in the seat so Randall wouldn't see her face and finally she let the tears come. Marc had let her go and her heart was breaking.

As the limo disappeared down the drive, Marc watched her go. She was unhappy and he wasn't happy, either, but he figured a lot of his sorrow was caused by the loss of his grandfather. He hated to see Lara go out of his life, but they had planned this from the beginning. He'd always intended to let her go, so why—he pulled up short as he corrected his thought. He never even *had* her to let her go.

He told himself that, given time, he'd settle back into the life he had before this crazy marriage of convenience, but right now, he wasn't happy. Lara had brought him joy and happiness. He hadn't stopped to think about the changes she had made in his life. Truthfully, he didn't want her to go, but there wasn't a choice. She wouldn't change and he didn't want to change. From the beginning they had planned this split. That's why she had been the perfect selection for his wife.

He walked back to his office, but he couldn't work. When he looked out the window all he saw was Lara in his arms, smiling and gazing up at him. "Dammit," he said aloud and stood impatiently. Maybe he just needed a few hours, a few days, and then he'd go back into his routine and go on with his life. He better, because she didn't have room in her plans for him. Right now, he hated to admit that he hurt. It shocked him, but he expected the pain of separation to go away.

Nine

Lara tried to keep busy, seeing her doctor, making appointments to talk to a counselor at the university about a doctorate. She still thought it would be best to put off starting medical school until her baby was six months or a year old. She needed a nursery in her house and needed to decide if she wanted to stay in the house she was in now.

She missed Marc every day, but she missed him at night even more. Her nights were empty, lonely, and it was difficult to sleep without him by her side. She knew that wasn't good for her or the baby.

She had another month to go on the courses she was currently enrolled in and then she would have

papers to write. She wanted to keep so busy she
didn't think about Marc, but that hadn't happened.
She thought about him constantly.

After being in her life each day and night, he was
suddenly gone out of it and she was having a difficult adjustment even though she was constantly busy.
Even if he had asked her to give up her career, which
he hadn't, could she? Absolutely not, because it was
too important to her. She might compromise, but she
still wanted to help people. Besides, Marc didn't love
her enough to ask. He didn't love her at all.

Soon he would be back, working at the office in
Dallas. Would she see him when he was in town?
She doubted it. They had gone their separate ways,
yet her heart had gone with him. She had known
from the first that she should guard her heart, but
how could she guard her heart against a man who
excited her more than anyone else ever had? Who
was sexier than any other man? Who was more fun
and considerate and a thousand other things that she
loved about him?

She couldn't. She hadn't. She'd fallen for him,
hard.

And the worst part was that she knew she'd love
him the rest of her life.

Marc spent the next week working at the ranch,
going to see his grandmother. Only one day did he

drive into Dallas and go by the office, but he was too aware that Lara was in Dallas.

He missed her in his bed at night. He missed her other times, missed her company, but nights were hell now and there was no quick, easy way to forget her.

He tried to forget her, but that was absolutely impossible. When his mother asked about her, he didn't tell his mother that Lara had moved back to Dallas and out of his life.

He hadn't started proceedings for the divorce. He had a great reluctance to do that and kept putting it off without really thinking about what he was doing.

One day he drove to Downly to see his mother at the restaurant at about ten in the morning because it would be quiet at that time. She was in her office and smiled when he entered.

"I'm glad you came to see me. I've been thinking about you and about Grandma. How's she doing?"

"She's doing okay. her companion that I hired to stay with her said she's handling losing Grandpa quite well. I helped her go through his things and we got that all sorted out."

Pilar wiped her eyes. "I miss him, but he wasn't going to get well. He was so happy that you married. He told me."

Marc felt a streak of guilt that Lara had already gone out of his life. "It made me happy, too, Mom. Lara liked him and he liked her. She told me she thought he was adorable, and I'm quoting her," he said, and his mother laughed.

"Adorable? Grandpa?" She laughed again. "I never thought of him that way. When he was young, he was always a force to be reckoned with. You're very much like him."

"Don't tell me that. I hope to heaven I never tell a grandson that he has to marry in a month."

She smiled. "He knew what he was doing. It worked out, didn't it? She's sweet and friendly, and you're happy and she seems happy. Actually, Marc, you've seemed much happier since your wedding. I think marriage is very good for you. Maybe it's being on the ranch, too."

"Lara told me that. She said I was happier than when I worked in town. I hadn't really thought about it," he said, thinking again that perhaps having Lara in his bed at night had been the real reason for his lightheartedness.

His mother grasped his hand. "You picked well, Marc. She's a wonderful young woman. Before you married, you told me that this was a marriage of convenience and she understood that. I hope you and Lara are not separating. I am so happy you're married and you'll be a father to her baby just as your dad was a father to you."

Marc felt another stab of guilt and wondered how he would ever break the news to his mother that he and Lara were divorcing now.

"Actually, Mom, Lara is very much like you. She's driven to go to medical school, if she's accepted, and become a doctor. If she doesn't get in medical school, she'll get a doctorate in chemistry. She wants to work in medical research because of losing her mother at such a young age. She feels that's a tribute to her Mom and it will help others. That's what drives her, just like you were driven to get this restaurant going."

"Marc, I had to do that because I had a baby and we needed to eat and have a roof over our heads. Your dad worked hard, but his health wasn't good."

"I know, Mom, but you went way beyond what you had to do. I used to want you at everything I did, my ball games, my programs at school, and I felt neglected when you missed something."

"Oh, Marc."

"I realize now that you came to most everything. You didn't miss the important events. And now I can understand why you worked like you did. Actually, Lara says I work hard. If I do, I got it from you. You were there for me always when it really mattered."

"I'm sorry I couldn't have been there one hundred percent of the time. I did the best I could."

"Which was wonderful." He smiled at her. "You still work hard."

"Now it's different, Marc. It keeps me busy. I still miss your dad and I need to keep busy."

"Lara is the same way you are. Her work is going to be her life, but then, my work is my life."

"Well, she has a noble goal—helping others, trying to find a medical cure and doing it for her mother. For so many reasons, I'm glad you married her. Her life will be good and so will yours. And so will mine with a grandchild." She squeezed his hand. "Marc, I can't wait. Grandpa was so happy about your marriage. You did the right thing."

Guilt swamped him. Even more, pain overtook him. The pain from realizing that he'd let Lara walk out of his life. For a moment it crossed his mind that he would be better off if he could get her back into it.

He thought about what his mother had said. Maybe she was right and he was looking at Lara's dedication to her career in the wrong way. He'd never thought about her noble motives. Till now.

He looked up at his mother. "You're a wonderful mom and I love you. And right now I better move along."

"Tell Lara hello."

"Sure, Mom. You take care of yourself," he said, kissing her cheek. He wasn't going to tell her yet about the divorce. He was in no hurry to get it and evidently Lara wasn't, either.

When he got into his car, he sat staring into the distance and seeing only Lara, remembering waking with her in his arms. How long would it take to forget her? *Maybe a lifetime* was the first answer that popped into mind. He grimaced and then realized he was still sitting in his car in front of his mother's restaurant. He started the car and drove away. It was a wonder she hadn't come out to see why he was still there.

Too many times during the day he was lost in thought about Lara. In her quiet way, she had wiggled into his life, and memories of her were everywhere at the ranch. He thought about spending the next week in Dallas at the office because it would get his mind off her. She didn't work there anymore. Whatever memories he had of her there were good memories of her as his secretary, quiet, in the background and not in his arms or in his bed. Maybe if he worked in the office, he could shake Lara the woman out of his thoughts.

He drove to the office and spent the day trying to catch up and get back into things there. To his dismay, too many times during the day he would realize he had stopped working and was lost in thought about Lara. Twice he got out his phone and looked at her number, wanting to call her and hear her voice.

Why was he missing her more instead of less, the longer she was gone?

He stood and went to the window to gaze out over the city of Dallas. She was out there somewhere, going to class or going to the doctor or at home studying. He pulled up his phone again and stared at it. What would it hurt to ask her to dinner? That was a simple thing. He was in town and he could catch up on what she was doing and how she was. What was the harm in sharing dinner?

He called her but she didn't answer. Was she out on a date? That thought made him unhappy and he knew that was ridiculous. He was going to divorce her. Of course she would go out with other men. But he didn't like that idea, no matter how he rationalized it.

Finding no peace at the office, he drove home to his Dallas mansion. But he didn't want to stay in a big empty house. Since when was he unhappy in his own home?

It was a chilly fall night with dark coming earlier now. He left and went to a drive-in and got a burger, taking a bite and then losing his appetite.

He couldn't stop thinking about her, but he had to. Either that or get her back into his life.

Could he live with her career if she was a doctor? Could he live with her work ethic? If it meant getting her back into his life, he could. He had made big mistakes, but that could change. For better or for worse, he was in love with his wife and he was wrong to try to get her to give up her career goals. She had unselfish, wonderful reasons for wanting the training she was trying to get. Far more lofty reasons for her hard work than he had.

He thought about himself and his own career. Was he happier at the ranch, as Lara said? He liked the competition and making deals in the corporate world, but was it worth it if he was uptight and not as happy?

With his inheritance and the money and business

he already had, he could get someone to run the office while he settled on the ranch and had a very good life. A good life if Lara was in it.

Why had he let her go? Why hadn't he realized he loved her?

The cattle ranch was a success, plus there was oil on his land. Could he rethink everything he thought he'd believed so he could have the woman he loved?

And he was in love. No doubt about it.

He groaned out loud and thought there was an old man in heaven chuckling about getting his grandson married off and settled on the ranch.

Now it was up to him. What was he going to do to win her back?

Marc stopped in Downly to see his mother. As he left the restaurant a pickup passed, stopped and backed up. Gabe Callahan got out of his truck and came striding toward him.

"Hey, buddy. What goes? You look like a man on a mission," Marc said, noting his friend's tight look and hooded eyes.

"I just saw you so I thought I'd stop. I ought to slug you."

"What the hell have I done? This sounds serious."

"When Meg is bothered about something, everyone is bothered about something."

"What are you talking about?"

"She told me that you and Lara have separated."

"I don't see that that's really much of your business."

"It's not, except it makes me angry. Lara's pregnant with your baby and you've left her." Gabe looked away and clenched his fists. "You know who that reminds me of, don't you?"

For the first time, Marc realized everyone would think exactly like Gabe—that he had left Lara when she was carrying his baby. And he wasn't going to deny it because of the promises he'd made to her.

"Don't even say it," Marc replied. "I know Lara didn't send you over here to get us back together."

"She didn't send me over here at all. I just wanted to tell you that I think that's rotten. And I'm going now. I've said what I wanted to say." He turned on his heel, but Marc stopped him.

"I know you mean well. And I intend to get us back together. I might have to do a little groveling."

"I should hope you would," Gabe said. "Look, I know I poked my nose in your business." He took a deep breath. "Just don't you dare be the damn dad I had."

"Under the circumstances, I can't get angry with you for that one. It was a mutual parting that we knew was coming, but I should have thought that one through." Marc ran a hand through his hair, struck hard by so many conflicting emotions. He didn't know how to navigate these waters, had never had to before. But in this moment he knew one thing he had to do.

He looked up at Gabe. "I want to tell you something. I've been over this with Lara to get her advice. She said to tell you. I wasn't going to, but Lara said family is the most important thing of all. My mom was supposed to never tell anyone this and she didn't—at least, not until after I married Lara and Mom found out Lara is pregnant."

"What in the hell are you talking about?"

"My mom was fifteen when she went to work for your family and lived in the house. She had me when she was sixteen."

"Yeah, the year my mother was pregnant with me. What—"

"Figure it out, Gabe." He knew his friend would connect the dots. He gave him time to put it all together. Their same ages, how much they looked alike.

He saw the moment it dawned on Gabe.

"That bastard father of mine," he spat out. "I'll damned. We're half brothers."

"As far as I'm concerned, Gabe, you can forget you ever learned the truth. You don't need to claim me as kin. My dad was John Medina. He was a wonderful dad and the only dad I want to acknowledge. Frankly, I'd just as soon bury this bit of information. We're grown men and we're best friends. That's good enough. But you have a right to know. Lara thought so."

"I'll think about it, and if I ever tell my family, I'll let you know. I may not even tell Meg. If you can live without all the Callahans knowing, I think I may just leave it that way."

"I'd be happy if you would. I don't like having to claim any relationship with your father."

"Yeah, I understand, and I appreciate you telling me. You're not missing much in the family doings. If you feel you need a big family because Lara doesn't have anyone, let me know and we'll get you into the family circle." He kicked his boot into the dust on the road. "Oh, hell. This is what I get for butting into your affairs. I'm going home." Gabe started walking back to his truck, then he suddenly stopped and turned around. "Don't ever be like him, Marc. You're a better man than that."

"Well, I wasn't for a while there, but I'm going to try to change that. Thanks, Gabe. You are a brother."

As Gabe drove away, Marc called Lara but she didn't answer again. He was just going to go camp on her doorstep because he wanted to straighten things out. Actually, he better apologize to her and see if she would take him back. He was so in love with her. How could he have been so blind and let her go?

He turned around to head to her house in Dallas. He was tempted to just go get her and take her home with him, but he was certain she would have her own ideas.

He banished the thought that floated at the edges of his mind. What if she wouldn't even let him back in her life?

Ten

As Lara walked through her living room, she saw a familiar car turn into her drive. Her heartbeat quickened, speeding again when she watched Marc come bounding up the drive, crossing her porch. Wearing jeans, a thick brown sweater, his boots and a black hat, he looked sexy, strong and so appealing. She rushed to open the door, but before she could speak, he swung her up into his arms and kissed her.

She wrapped her arms around him and held him, closing her eyes when his arms went around her. "I'm glad you're here."

He set her on her feet. "I have some big-time apologizing to do."

Perplexed, she stared at him. "Apologizing for what?" she asked, her heart beating even faster as surprise rocked her. "What are you doing here?"

He took her hands in his.

"First of all, I love you with all my heart."

His words took her breath away. "I've dreamed of hearing that from you, but we have—"

He put his finger lightly on her lips. "Listen to me. I love you and I apologize for being so damn bull-headed. You want to go to med school, I can support you. I hope I get to see you sometimes, but you're my wife and I want to keep right on being your husband."

"I can't believe what I'm hearing," she whispered, wondering what had happened in his life to cause such a change. Her heart raced. "You love me and you can accept it if I go to med school?"

"Yes, and if that doesn't work out, you'll get some kind of doctorate." He nodded at her and smiled. "I think that's fantastic. At least, I think it is if it keeps you in my life. Lara, I have been in hell without you. You brought me back into the world and then I let you slip away. Well, I guess I ran you off. I'm sorry. I've been such a fool. Will you forgive me and take me back?"

Her heart raced and she couldn't keep from laughing for joy. "Oh, Marc, of course I'll take you back. How can I not? You'll support my ambition and be a daddy to my baby."

"From now on, darlin', this is *our* baby. Okay?"

"I love you, Marc Medina. With all my heart."

"And I love you. After the baby comes, if we can work things out with your schedule, I'd like to move to the ranch permanently. I got to thinking about what you said and I am happier at the ranch. Would you like to live there?"

"Yes, if it's with you."

"With me and with our baby. I'll do anything I can to help you get into med school, to get the classes you need. You can go to your classes in the limo. Whatever it takes. I am so sorry I was so blind. I was about my mom. I was about you. Please forgive me."

"I love you and accept all apologies. I don't want to give it up, but what I've planned is to postpone going to school when the baby comes. I might take six months or I might take a year." She laughed. "We'll work it out. I'm not in a hurry, Marc."

"That's the best news possible, darlin'. I'll support whatever you want to do."

She laughed again. "I'll hold you to that one."

"I love you, Lara," he said solemnly. "I missed you and I never want to go through that agony again. I was incredibly wrong. I should never have let you go out of my life and I never will again. I've been in hell since you left, and this time I'm not letting you go."

"You won't have to. You have my love completely and you've had it for some time now." Her brows rose and she winked at him. "You're a little dense about love."

He grinned. "Maybe, but not about sex. Let me show you my talents."

He kissed her then, and she felt it all the way to her toes. And she felt his love, too.

Smiling, she looked up at him. "Am I dreaming? I can't believe this is happening."

"Believe it, darlin'."

"You know, little towns need doctors, too. I could live on the ranch and probably work in some small town out near Downly."

"Whatever makes you happy and keeps you married to me."

"I'll be married to you forever," she said. "Oh, how I love you." She laughed before she stood on tiptoe to kiss him. She paused to look up at him.

"Marc, I think your grandpa knew what he was doing."

Marc shook his head. "He probably did. He probably figured I'd find someone I'd love, and when I started living on the ranch, I wouldn't want to leave it. He was a crafty fellow and managed to get his way a lot."

"I'm glad I got to know him, even that little bit."

"By the way, I told Gabe about my bloodline. He wants to bury that bit of info, which is just fine with me. I'm happy with his friendship. Actually, I'm friends with all the Callahan brothers and that's good enough."

"I'm so happy," she said. She clung tightly to him,

joyous and looking forward to the future. She leaned away and flashed her hand at him. Her diamond ring sparkled. "See, I'm still wearing my wedding band and I'm still married to you. I wasn't going to take that off until that divorce was final."

"It will never be final. You're mine forever, sweetie. I love you more than I can tell you."

He kissed her then, pulling her tightly to him and leaning over her. She clung to him while happiness made her tremble. She would have Marc in her life, her new little baby, and someday, she would be able to work somewhere to help sick people feel better as a tribute to her mother.

She leaned away and placed her hand on his cheek.

"I want to spend a lifetime showing you how much I love you."

"Sounds like a good deal to me. Come here, my sweet wife."

She smiled at him. Then she closed her eyes as he kissed her.

He framed her face with his hands. "I love you, Lara. From now on I'll spend every minute of my life trying to make you happy."

She hugged him. "You've made me so happy already." She leaned back and looked into his eyes. "A couple of years from now, I want to be pregnant with *your* baby. I love you, Marc. I love you now and forever."

She stood on tiptoe to kiss him as he wrapped his arms around her and held her tightly. Joy filled her and she knew the biggest fortune she had was his love that she would treasure all her life. A life filled with his love and their children.

* * * * *

If you liked this story of love beneath the Texan skies, pick up these other CALLAHAN'S CLAN *novels from* USA TODAY *bestselling author Sara Orwig!*

EXPECTING THE RANCHER'S CHILD
THE RANCHER'S NANNY BARGAIN
THE RANCHER'S CINDERELLA BRIDE

And don't miss her other great Western romances!

TEXAS-SIZED TEMPTATION
THE TEXAN'S FORBIDDEN FIANCÉE

Available now from Harlequin Desire!

***

If you're on Twitter, tell us what you think of Harlequin Desire! #harlequindesire

SPECIAL EXCERPT FROM

HQN™

Ready or not, love will find a way,
even when confronted with the most reluctant of hearts...

Read on for a sneak peek of the next
GUTHRIE BROTHERS *book, WORTH THE WAIT,*
from New York Times *bestselling author Lori Foster!*

Violet, looking messier than Hogan had ever seen her, was leaning over the papers again scattered across her desk.

"Violet?"

Slowly she turned her face toward him.

Her bloodshot eyes surprised him. Sick. He stepped in farther. "Hey, you okay?"

She looked from him to the paperwork. "I don't know." More coughs racked her.

Hogan strode forward and put a hand to her forehead. "Shit. You're burning up."

"What time is it?"

"A few minutes after midnight."

"Oh." She pushed back from the desk but didn't make it far. "The restaurant," she gasped in between strained breaths.

"I took care of it." Holding her elbow, he helped to support her as she stood. His most pressing thought was getting her home and in bed. No, not the way he'd like, but definitely the way she needed. "Where are your car keys?"

Unsteady on her feet, she frowned. "What do you mean, you took care of it?"

"You have good employees—you know that. They're aware of the routine. Colt pitched in, too. Everything is done."

"But…"

"I double-checked. I'm not incompetent, so trust me."

Her frown darkened.

"You can thank me, Violet."

She tried to look stern, coughed again and gave up. "Thank you." Still she kept one hand on the desk. "I'm just so blasted tired."

"I know." He eased her into his side, his arm around her. "Come on. Let me drive you home." Then he found her purse and without a qualm, dug through it for her keys.

He found them. He also found two condoms. His gaze flashed to hers, but her eyes were closed and she looked asleep on her feet, her body utterly boneless as she drew in shallow, strained breaths.

"Come on." With an arm around her, her purse and keys held in his free hand, he led her out the back way to the employee lot, securing the door behind her. Her yellow Mustang shone bright beneath security lights.

His bike would be okay. Or at least, it better be.

Violet tried to get herself together but it wasn't easy. She honestly felt like she could close her eyes and nod right off. "The trash—"

"Was taken out." He opened the passenger door and helped her in.

"If you left on even one fan—"

"It would set off the security sensors. I know. They're all off." He fastened her seat belt around her and closed her door.

As soon as he slid behind the wheel, she said, "But the end-of-day reports—"

"Are done." He started her car. "Try not to worry, okay?"

Easier said than done.

Because the town was so small, Hogan seemed to know where she lived even though she'd never had him over. She hadn't dared.

Hogan in her home? Nope. Not a good idea.

Even feeling miserable, her head pounding and her chest aching, she was acutely aware of him beside her in the enclosed car, and the way he kept glancing at her. He tempted her, always had, from the first day she'd met him.

He was also a major runaround. Supposedly a reformed runaround, but she didn't trust in that. Things had happened with his late wife, things that had made him bitter and unpredictable.

Yet no less appealing.

She wasn't one to pry; otherwise she might have gotten all the details from Honor, his sister-in-law, already. She figured if he ever wanted to, Hogan himself would tell her. Not that there was any reason, since she would not get involved with him.

Hogan was fun to tease, like watching the flames in a bonfire. You watched, you enjoyed, but you did not jump in the fire. She needed Hogan Guthrie, but she wasn't a stupid woman, so she tried to never court trouble.

Don't miss WORTH THE WAIT
by New York Times *bestselling author Lori Foster!*

EXCLUSIVE LIMITED TIME OFFER AT
www.HARLEQUIN.com

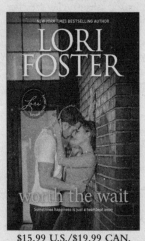

NEW YORK TIMES BESTSELLING AUTHOR

LORI FOSTER

worth the wait

Sometimes happiness is just a heartbeat away

$15.99 U.S./$19.99 CAN.

$1.⁵⁰ OFF

New York Times Bestselling Author

LORI FOSTER

worth the wait

Ready or not...
love will find a way

Available July 25, 2017.
Get your copy today!

Receive **$1.50 OFF** the purchase price of
WORTH THE WAIT by Lori Foster
when you use the coupon code below on Harlequin.com.

LFWORTHIT

Offer valid from July 25, 2017, until August 31, 2017, on www.Harlequin.com.

Valid in the U.S.A. and Canada only. To redeem this offer, please add the print
or ebook version of WORTH THE WAIT by Lori Foster to your shopping cart and
then enter the coupon code at checkout.

HQN™

www.HQNBooks.com

PHCOUPLFHD0817